LUIGI FERRO
DEATH BEHIND THE SCENES

Luigi Ferro
Death Behind the Scenes
Story by Matt Borne
Copyright © 2023
Cover by Mats Ingelborn
Photos by A.Karnaushenko, Kiuikson & Wirestock
ISBN print: 978-91-89822-40-5
ISBN e-book: 978-91-89822-41-2
Published by Yabot AB, Sweden, 2023

1

The dim glow of a solitary lamp cast shadows on the peeling wallpaper of my office. Worn leather furniture sighed under the weight of secrets and betrayals, bearing witness to countless confessions and revelations. The faint scent of tobacco clung to every surface, lingering like the memories of past cases that refused to be forgotten. I quit smoking several years ago but allowed my clients to puff to ease their tensions. Amidst this familiar gloom, the soft sounds of intimate lovemaking whispered, blending with the muted hum of the small city four floors down at San Marino's Piazza della Libertà.

Her large brown eyes, dark as night, gazed into mine with a smoldering intensity as I traced the contour of her jaw with my fingertips. Her skin was smooth as silk beneath my touch as if she were sculpted from the finest Italian marble. She lay back on the couch, inviting me to explore further, the fabric of her 1950s-style dress rustling against the worn leather. I followed her, my lips finding the graceful curve of her neck, eliciting a breathy sigh that sent a shiver down my spine. Her name was Caterina, and she had called me an hour ago, interrupting my boredom by luring me toward the depths of temptation.

"Luigi," she breathed, her hands resting on my chest, "you have no idea what you do to me."

I smirked, my fingers slipping beneath the hem of

her dress, gently grazing her thigh. "Oh, Caterina, I think I have some idea," I replied, my voice barely above a whisper.

As our bodies entwined, our desires fueled by the secrecy of an office rendezvous, I couldn't help but wonder how it had come to this. The sultry temptress beneath me was both my salvation and my undoing, a living embodiment of the power struggle that defined our lives. It seemed that fate had a cruel sense of humor, throwing us together in a dance of seduction and deception, each vying for control even as we succumbed to the irresistible pull of our shared passion.

Caterina was a struggling composer, doing odd pieces for commercials and film, but it was as a weather girl on SMTV that she made ends meet.

"Luigi," she purred, her breath hot against my ear. "You're quite the detective, aren't you?"

"Only when it comes to uncovering hidden treasures," I murmured, my fingers tracing the curve of her ankle, feeling the heat of her body through the thin nylons. It was a game we played – coy and full of innuendo. We both knew where the night would lead us, but the anticipation only heightened our senses, sharpening our appetites.

At that moment, as I bent over and kissed her shin, I was reminded of the words of an old Italian proverb: "He who kisses the feet of his beloved is not without sin." And in that moment, I was a sinner – but what sweet sin it was.

Her laughter rang out like silver bells, her dark hair

spilling over her shoulders as she arched her back. "Is that what you think I am? A treasure to be discovered?"

"Sure," I replied, brushing a stray lock of hair from her face, tucking it behind her ear. "Some things are worth the chase."

"Ah, Luigi," she sighed, her voice a sultry mix of pleasure and satisfaction.

As our lips met again, I couldn't help but feel an odd twinge of guilt at the back of my mind. It wasn't the first time I'd given in to temptation, nor would it be the last, but somehow, this felt different. Perhaps it was the way she looked at me, as though she saw straight through to the man I was underneath – a man who craved power, control, and the thrill of the chase.

"Tell me, Luigi," she whispered between kisses, her nails digging into my shoulders. "What do you truly desire?"

"Right now?" I asked my voice husky with need. "I desire nothing more than to get lost in this moment."

"Then let's get lost together," she breathed, pulling me closer.

The shrill ringing of my cell phone cut through the haze of desire that had enveloped us. Caterina stiffened in my arms, her wide eyes meeting mine as if questioning whether I would dare to answer it. In that instant, I knew that I couldn't ignore the call. If it was a client, I needed the business. The last few weeks had been dry. With a reluctant sigh, I pulled away from her, feeling the loss of warmth and the sudden emptiness that came with it.

"Excuse me, amore," I murmured as I reached for

the device on the nearby desk. I could feel her gaze still locked on me, silently pleading for me to return to our activities. But there was something about the call – something urgent, insistent, that told me I needed to answer it.

"Pronto," I said gruffly into the receiver, my voice betraying my frustration at the intrusion.

"Signor Ferro," a hushed voice replied, trembling and breathless. A woman's voice, unfamiliar yet somehow haunting, like a siren's song beckoning me towards the unknown. "I need your help."

"Who is this?" I asked, my curiosity piqued despite my better judgment.

"My name is Tilda Larsson. I am Valeria Bianchi's personal assistant," she whispered, her words rushed and desperate. "It's urgent, please."

I could scarcely believe my ears - Valeria Bianchi, the famous actress, seeking my services? It was a notion as intoxicating as the woman who lay sprawled across the worn leather couch before me. Valeria Bianchi had captured the hearts of men across Italy, myself included, and the rest of the world. How could I refuse such a request? A chance to step into her world was an opportunity I could not pass up.

"So," I relented, cursing myself for abandoning Caterina so readily. "What do you need?"

"Signora Bianchi needs you," she blurted out, her voice cracking with the weight of the revelation. "She needs your expertise in a delicate matter…"

My curiosity piqued, I sat up straighter, the sensuous

atmosphere of my office suddenly replaced by an air of urgency. "What's going on?"

"Signora Bianchi is being blackmailed. She's terrified, and she needs your expertise."

"Blackmailed?" I echoed, "Very well, Signorina Larsson, I'll take the case. Tell me everything. Who's blackmailing her?"

"Please, Signor Ferro... I can't talk about it over the phone. Can you meet Signora Bianchi immediately?"

"Very well," I replied, my heart racing at the prospect of meeting the woman who had intoxicated me from afar with her sultry performances on the silver screen. "Where do we meet?"

"Her rented beach house, at Lido di Dante, north of Rimini," Tilda's voice was barely audible; her words rushed as if trying to outrun the fear that clung to them.

"Expect me there," I told her, the gravity of the situation not lost on me. The line went dead, leaving me with a mixture of anticipation and dread.

"Who was that?" Caterina asked, her voice tinged with jealousy as she tried to read my expression.

"Business, dear," I replied evasively, unwilling to divulge the true nature of the call. "I'm afraid our evening must be cut short."

"Will I see you again?" she inquired, her eyes searching mine for reassurance.

"Of course," I murmured, pulling her close for one final kiss before stepping away, my thoughts already consumed by the mysterious circumstances that awaited me.

As I left the warmth of my office behind, I couldn't help but feel the cold tendrils of uncertainty slithering through my veins, coiling around my heart like the weight of an unspoken secret. Little did I know just how deep this web of deceit would lead me or the darkness that lurked within its shadows.

*

The journey to Lido di Dante was a study in contrasts. My Vespa hummed beneath me as I navigated through the bustling streets of San Marino, weaving between cars and tourists alike. The scent of fresh tomato sauce and strong espresso filled the air, mingling with the cacophony of voices speaking animatedly in their native tongue.

As the city faded into the distance, the landscape transformed before my eyes. Rolling hills gave way to gently sloping dunes, and the once-distant sea now stretched out before me like a vast expanse of azure silk. The salty breeze caressed my face as I approached the secluded beach house, its whitewashed walls gleaming in the sunlight like the exposed bones of some ancient leviathan.

I killed the engine of my Vespa and dismounted, taking a moment to appreciate the serene beauty that surrounded me. The coastal air embraced me as I approached the beach house. The waves crashed against the shore with an insistent rhythm, their foamy crests glittering like shattered glass under the afternoon sun. Seagulls wheeled overhead, their raucous cries weaving a tapestry of sound that was at once familiar and unsettling.

I hastened my steps towards the house, eager to unravel the mystery that awaited me within its walls. As I neared the entrance, I caught a glimpse of Valeria through the large windows, her lithe silhouette framed by the golden rays that filtered through the gauzy curtains. Even from this distance, I could see the tension that marred her otherwise flawless features. She paced the room like a caged animal, her movements graceful yet frenetic.

Suddenly, the tranquility of the scene was shattered by the deafening crack of a gunshot. My heart leaped into my throat as I instinctively threw myself against the wall, adrenaline coursing through my veins like liquid fire. For a moment, all I could hear was the ragged sound of my own breath, as though the world outside had ceased to exist.

"Signora Bianchi!" I shouted, my voice barely audible above the pounding of my heart. I forced myself to move, propelling my body through the door and into the chaos that greeted me on the other side.

The room was a tableau of shock and disbelief. Valeria stood in the center, her delicate hand still gripping the smoking gun. Her eyes were wide with terror, their emerald depths reflecting the horror of what she had done. A man lay sprawled on the floor, his lifeblood seeping into the plush carpet beneath him.

"What have you done?" I asked, my voice barely a whisper as I took in the scene before me. My mind raced, trying to make sense of the carnage that had so suddenly erupted into this oasis of serenity.

"I had no choice," she stammered, her eyes never leaving the lifeless form. "He threatened me, said he would destroy everything I've worked for if I didn't give in to his demands."

"Put down the gun, Signora Bianchi," I commanded, my tone firm yet gentle. She hesitated for a moment, then complied, her hand trembling as the weapon clattered to the floor. I moved closer, my senses acutely aware of the scent of gunpowder and the metallic tang of blood that hung in the air.

Then her eyes found me and saw me for the first time.

"Who are you?" she said, frowning.

"My name is Luigi Ferro, private investigator," I replied, extending my hand to greet her, but she did not take it. "Your assistant, Miss Larsson, called me. You needed my services…"

She shrugged. "Not anymore."

It seemed impossible that the man who had been blackmailing Valeria now lay dead before me, the finality of his demise etched into the stillness of his body.

"But, there may be other ways you can assist, Signor Ferro," she continued, her voice barely audible above the roar of the waves outside, and moved her gaze to the lifeless body on the floor. "Help me make this go away."

As I looked into her eyes, I saw the desperation that lay beneath the surface like a dormant volcano, threatening to erupt at any moment. It was at that instant that I realized the true danger of the situation. The tangled web of secrets and lies weaved around Valeria now threatened to ensnare us both, trapping us in its deadly embrace.

"Signora Bianchi, I will do what I can," I assured her, my words heavy with the weight of the decision I had just made. "But first, we need to understand what has happened here."

"I can't let the police find out about this," Valeria implored, her chest heaving with each ragged breath.

"Signor Bianchi," I started, my voice firm but sympathetic, "I understand that you're afraid, and you have every reason to be. But covering up a murder –"

"Self-defense!" she interjected, desperation lacing her words.

"Even so," I continued, "covering up a death won't make your problems disappear. In fact, it will only create more questions and more suspicion. You must face this head-on and let the authorities handle it."

As I spoke, I could see the anguish in her eyes, the dilemma tearing her apart from within like a voracious beast gnawing at her soul. She clutched the fabric of her dress tightly as if seeking solace in its delicate threads. The scent of the sea drifted into the room, mingling with the acrid stench of gunpowder, creating a dissonant symphony that mirrored the chaos that had erupted in our lives.

"Alright, Ferro," she conceded, her voice barely audible above the crashing waves outside. "But promise me you'll be by my side throughout this ordeal. I don't know if I can face it alone."

"Of course," I assured her, placing a reassuring hand on her shoulder. Her skin was cold, trembling beneath my touch like an autumn leaf caught in a gust of wind. "I'll do everything in my power to help you."

"Thank you," she whispered, her voice trembling with gratitude and unspoken fear. I could see a glimmer of hope returning to her tear-filled eyes, a flickering flame struggling to stay alight amidst a storm of darkness.

"Who was this man?" I asked.

"He wasn't a man," she retorted, her voice laced with scorn. "He was a leech, a human parasite."

"But, I guess he had a name?"

"Si, Franco Carter. American!" She almost spat out the words.

"And he was blackmailing you?"

She nodded her head in silence, the blonde tresses flowing as if in slow motion. She was beautiful, even in distress.

"What did he have over you?"

"Immaterial now," she shrugged.

"Because he's six feet under?"

"Precisely, Signor Ferro."

Blood pooled around Franco Carter's lifeless body, a macabre Rorschach test that painted the floor in shades of crimson. My nostrils flared as I took in the metallic tang of blood mingling with the salty sea air. It was an olfactory juxtaposition that would linger long after the memory of our conversation had faded.

"Stay here," I instructed Valeria, my voice low and steady, betraying none of the conflict raging within me. "I need a moment."

As I stepped away from her, I felt the heavy weight of her gaze follow me, a silent plea for absolution that I wasn't certain I could give. The room seemed to close in on me, each breath laced with the scent of death and the secrets it kept hidden.

My eyes scanned the surroundings, lingering on the shattered glass that lay scattered like fallen stars across the polished wooden floorboards. The windowpane had given way under the force of the bullet, surrendering its structural integrity as easily as Valeria had surrendered her own.

I knelt beside Carter's body, studying the gunshot wound with a practiced eye. I couldn't help but feel a pang of sympathy for the man – after all, we had both succumbed to Valeria's irresistible allure. But sympathy was a luxury I couldn't afford in my line of work.

"Were you working for someone, Carter?" I muttered under my breath as I examined the dead man's pockets, finding nothing but a crumpled pack of cigarettes and a tarnished silver lighter engraved with the initials 'F.C.' No wallet, no identification – only more questions.

The room seemed to exhale as we sealed our clandestine pact, the air pregnant with the unspoken knowledge that our fates were now irrevocably entwined. I moved from one corner of the room to another, my keen eyes searching for any detail that might offer a glimpse into the twisted machinations of Franco Carter's mind.

"What did he threaten you with?" I asked, my voice barely more than a whisper.

Valeria hesitated before responding, the weight of her words almost tangible. "He knew things... things that could ruin me."

"Things" hung in the air between us, heavy and laden with implications I dared not entertain. For now, though, it was enough to know that there was something worth fighting for – a secret worth protecting.

"Let's call Commissario Carlotto," I suggested, my fingers reaching for the phone in my pocket. I hesitated, feeling the weight of the consequences that would follow from our next actions.

"No, please, Signor Ferro. Please don't." Valeria's trembling hands wiped away the tears cascading down her cheeks, leaving behind streaks of sorrowful mascara. Her large eyes, filled with an intoxicating blend of fear and relief, locked onto mine as she struggled to find her voice.

The wind from the sea swept through the room, the thin curtains twirling as if in a dance. She stood with a subtle grace, even though her posture was riddled with undeniable panic. The faintest touch of moonlight illuminated the edges of her profile, casting an ethereal glow against her alabaster skin. There was vulnerability in her eyes but a determined set to her jaw.

"Signor Ferro, listen," Valeria began, her voice trembling yet silken, lacing each syllable with an intimate urgency. "I implore you to understand. Franco Carter was not an innocent. He haunted my every step, leveraged shadows from my past, intending to drag me into the abyss. Sure, you've seen the complexities of our world. Can you not empathize with a moment of profound desperation?"

I felt the weight of her gaze, the very core of me ensnared by those deep, cerulean orbs brimming with a cocktail of fear and defiance. I shifted uneasily, fingers brushing the cold steel of the phone in my pocket.

"It isn't just about Carter," she continued her voice barely above a whisper, moving closer. "There are... entanglements, depths you cannot fathom. If you bring the police into this sordid tapestry, it won't be only me that's ensnared."

I raised an eyebrow. "So, you're suggesting a DIY funeral, are you?"

She paused, mere inches from me now. "Trust in our shared discretion. In the shadows of the night, we both operate, albeit on different planes. I ask not for forgiveness but for understanding. For once, let the web of intrigue serve to protect rather than ensnare."

I looked into her eyes, searching for deceit but finding a desperate authenticity.

"Can you tell me exactly what happened here tonight?" I ventured.

She moved in even closer; the intoxicating blend of her perfume, a rich tapestry of Tuscan flowers and Roman nights, filled the space between us. Her eyes held a world of secrets and promises, and for a moment, I was lost in them, drowning in a sea of amber temptation.

Her fingers, delicate but with a strength that spoke of her life's hardships, traced a line up my arm, making my senses buzz with electricity. The contours of her face were highlighted by the dim ambient light, each feature sculpted as if by a master artist.

"Ferro," she whispered, her voice sultry, dripping with intent, "you've seen the world's ugliness. Tonight, let's forget it."

Drawn to her like a moth to a flame, I leaned in, caught in the riptide of her allure. Just as our lips were about to meet, an unexpected force crashed against my skull. The world spun, and the last thing I remember before the consuming darkness was the feeling of betrayal, underscored by Valeria's haunting gaze.

2

A sharp shake jolted me awake. A bright ray of sunlight pierced mercilessly through my eyelids. My mind raced to catch up, wading through the muddle of memories. There was a pounding in my head with the weight of a thousand hammers, and for a moment, I couldn't remember where I was.

"Signore Ferro!" The voice was urgent, almost frantic. My eyes adjusted and found a young woman hovering above me, her blonde hair cascading down her shoulders like golden silk. Her pale blue eyes seemed to hold secrets, and her red lips curved into a knowing smile that sent shivers down my spine. She was dressed in a figure-hugging dress that left little to the imagination, and despite the disorientation clouding my thoughts, I couldn't help but feel drawn to her.

"Who are you?" I asked, my voice hoarse.

"Ah, scusi. I am Tilda Larsson," she replied, her words laced with the lilting melody of a Swedish accent. "I am Signora Bianchi's personal assistant."

"What–" I began, still trying to grasp my bearings.

"There's no time," she whispered, urgency dripping from each syllable. The silken sheets that enveloped me were a far cry from the humble fabric of my own abode. It all came back in flashes – the beach house, the dead blackmailer, Valeria's smoky eyes promising everything and nothing.

"Where's Valeria?" My voice was rough, remnants of being knocked out, making it gravelly.

Tilda bit her red lip, the weight of secrets apparent in her tense posture. Despite her evident anxiety, she was still impossibly beautiful, her figure-hugging dress accentuating every curve. "We need to leave. Now," she pressed.

But first, I needed answers.

I sat up, rubbing my temples, trying to piece together the events from last night.

Tilda had rang my office and requested me to meet Valeria Bianchi at her rented beach house. I had driven down and met Valeria as she shot and killed Franco Carter, the assumed blackmailer. Then I had a memory of Valeria's silky smooth skin, mesmerizing eyes, and her delicate perfume before I was struck down by someone. Was it Valeria?

"Where is she?" I questioned.

Tilda placed a slender finger against her lips, her gaze locked onto mine. "Signor Ferro, I need you to focus," Tilda urged, her eyes wide with concern. "Signora Bianchi has been kidnapped."

"Kidnapped?" I repeated, my heart lurching in my chest. The words hit me like a punch to the gut, their implications far more sinister than I could have anticipated.

"Si," Tilda confirmed, wringing her hands together nervously. "I received an anonymous phone call some half hour ago. I rushed here to see if she was here, but I only found you. Do you know where she is, Signor Ferro? What did you two do last night?"

"Did they want money? Any other demands?" I asked, avoiding to answer. My instincts told me this was no ordinary kidnapping but something far more calculated.

"I don't know," she admitted, shaking her head. "But we must act quickly. We can't afford to waste any time."

"Alright," I agreed, pushing through the haze of confusion that clouded my thoughts. I forced myself to focus on the matter at hand, knowing that Valeria's life hung in the balance. "Tell me everything you know about the call, and let's figure out our next move."

As Tilda relayed the details of the call, her voice wavering with fear, I couldn't help but feel an overwhelming sense of responsibility for Valeria's safety. Though our relationship had been complicated by desire and temptation, there was no denying the bond we shared. And now, it was up to me to save her from the clutches of an unknown enemy.

While Tilda spoke, I took note of her body language – the way her fingers fiddled with the hem of her dress, betraying her nervousness, the subtle tremble in her voice as she recounted the threat. There was something undeniably seductive about the way she carried herself, even in a moment of crisis. It was both captivating and unnerving.

"Signor Ferro," Tilda's voice broke through my reverie, her expression pleading. "Will you help me? Will you help find Signora Bianchi?"

"Of course," I replied without hesitation. If it was because I wanted to help this Scandinavian beauty with anything or if I actually cared about the actress who hit me on the head, I did not know… ”We'll find her, Tilda. I promise, but only if you call me Luigi.”

”Thank you,” she breathed, relief washing over her features like a balm. Though the shadows of fear still lingered in her eyes, there was a newfound determination simmering beneath the surface.

”Let's get to work,” I said, struggling out of bed, my head still pounding like an old set of pistons. ”Have you searched the house?”

Tilda went to the room next door and I started where I was. My fingers lingered with reluctant hesitance over the sleek, lacquered surface of the dresser. The act of rifling through Valeria Bianchi's belongings felt like a trespass, an invasion into a private realm where secrets lay draped in silk and whispers. My profession, though it often skirted the edges of other people's lives, seldom delved so deeply into their personal sanctuaries. Yet here I was, driven by a need for answers, wading through the intimate artifacts of Valeria's life.

As I opened the drawer, the musty scent of perfume wafted up, an aroma that spoke of hidden depths and long-buried truths. Nestled among the delicate laces and fine fabrics, my fingers stumbled upon a photograph. It was of a young woman, her blonde hair cascading like a golden waterfall over bare, alabaster shoulders, her pose unabashedly pornographic. The image was stark, raw – a vivid contrast to the elegant opulence of Valeria's public persona.

For a fleeting moment, I found myself ensnared in the web of the photo's implications. Could the celebrated Valeria Bianchi, the siren who haunted the dreams of countless men, be drawn to women? The thought skittered across my mind, an uncomfortable intruder that I hastened to dismiss. It felt like prying into a chapter of her life that was not mine to read, a story where I had no place.

With a shake of my head, as if to dislodge the discomfiting thought, I carefully replaced the photo, ensuring it lay exactly as it had been. I closed the drawer with a soft click, a quiet end to a silent intrusion, my heart still thudding unevenly in my chest.

The image of the blonde woman etched behind my eyelids, as I went downstairs to join Tilda.

The sun was high in the blue morning sky, and the sea glittered invitingly in the east. As I stood in the doorway of the living room, my mind raced as I looked around. The lifeless body of Franco Carter was gone. The shattered window pane replaced, and no traces of shattered glass or blood… The room has been thoroughly cleaned – or was my memory failing me? The tendrils of twilight crept through my brain, bringing with them a palpable sense of tension and unease. Maybe I was struck down as Valeria was abducted?

"Where would they take her?" Tilda asked, her voice barely audible above the hum of the city. I could see the desperation in her eyes – a raw, almost primal fear that cut straight to my core.

"Right now, I don't know," I admitted, my gaze sweeping across the room. "But I'm going to find out."

With each passing moment, the mystery surrounding

Valeria's disappearance deepened. It was as if she had vanished into thin air, leaving nothing behind but a trail of unanswered questions and a lingering sense of dread. And yet, there was one thing that gnawed at me more than anything else: the absence of Franco Carter's body and any evidence of his involvement in the crime. Maybe Carter was working for someone who swept up the pieces?

Taking a deep breath, I drew my phone from my pocket and dialed the number of a man whose assistance I hoped would be invaluable – Commissario Gastone Carlotto of the Rimini crime squad. The line rang once, twice, before his gravelly voice answered on the other end.

"Carlotto."

"Commissario, it's Luigi Ferro. I've got a situation that needs your expertise."

"Ah, the private detective," he said, his tone dripping with skepticism. "What mess have you found yourself in this time, Signore?"

"Valeria Bianchi, the actress, has been kidnapped, and I'm trying to track her down. There's more to this case than meets the eye, and I think you might have some insights."

"Kidnapped?" Carlotto's voice softened slightly, but the distrust was still palpable. "Where was she last seen?"

"I saw her last at her villa in Lido di Dante, but I am not sure she was taken from here — there are no signs of battle or struggle…"

"Is that where she's staying?" Carlotto grunted.

Tilda shook her head and pointed to a keycard in her hand.

"No, Commissario," I replied. "She is staying at the Grand Hotel Rimini."

"Then, I'll meet you there, prima possibile!"

*

The dim light of the Grand Hotel Rimini's opulent lobby cast flickering shadows on the walls, where portraits of bygone starlets and faded aristocrats gazed down upon us with a mixture of envy and disdain. The air was heavy with the scent of expensive perfume and the distant echo of whispered secrets as if the very walls themselves were privy to the hidden dramas that unfolded within.

"Quite a place," I murmured, taking in the grand staircase and the extravagant chandeliers that dripped crystals like icicles of frozen time.

"Indeed," Tilda agreed, her voice soft and seductive as a siren's song. "And not without its share of secrets."

Commissario Carlotto, who had arrived moments before us, stood stiffly beside us, his eyes constantly scanning the room for any sign of danger or deceit. I could sense his unease, the way he seemed almost repelled by the decadence that surrounded us. But then again, he and I had never seen eye to eye on much.

"Let's get down to business, shall we?" he said with a wry smile, extending his hand reluctantly.

"Fine by me," I replied, shaking his hand with equal hesitation.

Tilda and I gave Carlotto the details up to this point,

as much as we knew, or in my case, as much as I wanted him to know, leaving out the shooting, the blackmail, and the dead man. Carlotto's brow furrowing with each passing moment.

"Something doesn't add up here, Ferro," he mused, eyes narrowing in suspicion. "I know you're not one for playing by the rules, but we need to tread carefully. This case is like a viper waiting to strike – make one wrong move, and it'll be our necks on the line."

"Trust me, Commissario," I said, my voice barely more than a whisper. "I want to find Valeria just as much as you do. But we have to work together if we're going to untangle this mess."

"Alright, Ferro," he conceded, a hint of begrudging respect in his voice. "But don't think for a second that I won't be keeping a close eye on you."

"Wouldn't expect anything less," I replied, my determination renewed. Together, we began to unravel the threads of deceit that bound us all in this dangerous game of desire, betrayal, and power.

"Let's not waste any more time," Carlotto said curtly, gesturing for us to bring him towards Valeria Bianchi's suite. "We have a job to do, and I don't intend to linger here any longer than necessary."

As we made our way through the corridors, I couldn't help but feel a certain thrill at the prospect of working alongside my longtime rival. Though I knew I could never fully trust him, there was something exhilarating about the tension that crackled between us like an electric current.

"Here we are," Tilda announced, stopping suddenly

　　　　　　　　　　　　　　　　

in front of a door adorned with golden filigree. "Signora Bianchi's suite."

I raised an eyebrow. "Let's see what it has to offer."

Tilda hesitated, biting her lower lip as she fumbled with the key. "Remember, Ferro," she whispered, her blue eyes locked on mine with an intensity that made my heart skip a beat. "We're doing this for Valeria."

"Of course," I replied, trying to ignore the way her gaze seemed to bore straight through me. "She's all that matters."

The door swung open to reveal a room that was every bit as lavish as the rest of the hotel, but with an air of intimacy that spoke of private desires and forbidden pleasures. It was a place where secrets were born, and dreams took flight, only to be crushed beneath the weight of reality.

"Let's get to work," Carlotto said, his voice barely audible above the rustle of silk curtains and the distant murmur of unseen lovers. "Time is of the essence when dealing with a missing person."

Together, we began our search for clues, each of us lost in our own thoughts as we sifted through the remnants of Valeria's life. As the minutes passed and the whispers grew louder, I couldn't help but wonder what other secrets lay hidden within these walls, just waiting to be uncovered.

The absence of evidence gnawed at my insides like a parasite, leaving me with an unsettling sense of foreboding. I knew that time was of the essence, and my instincts told me that it was all too neat. The cleaned-up beach villa, the tidy hotel suite, and a missing actress – I could not uncover this dark web of lies alone.

”Luigi?” Tilda whispered, her fingers brushing against my arm as we searched the room. ”Do you think they hurt her?”

”I don't know,” I replied softly, my heart twisting in my chest at the thought. ”Let's focus on finding her first.”

The door to Valeria Bianchi's suite swung again, interrupting the simmering tension in the air. First to enter was a bold and muscular figure in an ill-fitting suit. His presence immediately filled the room like a thundercloud, his dark eyes scanning the scene with practiced vigilance. His bulky frame, a testament to many hours spent pushing iron, moved with surprising grace for a man of his size.

Behind him, a contrast in every sense, slipped in a second figure. This man was short, slim, and wiry, his frame gaunt as if carved from old wood. His hair, peppered with gray, gave him a distinguished look, yet there was a sharpness in his eyes that suggested a mind ever calculating. Though lacking stature, he carried himself with an air of authority that immediately commanded attention.

As he stepped further into the light, I recognized him. ”Daniel Hallstrom,” I murmured to myself, barely audible over the muted tension of the room. The renowned film director currently working with Valeria Bianchi in the Emilia-Romagna Studios.

”Where is she? She has not shown up today!”

Hallstrom barked, searching the room for Valeria or at least an answer.

”She is missing, Signor Hallstrom,” Tilda said.

”Missing? What do you mean, missing?”

”And who are you two?” asked Commissario Carlotto, eyeing the newcomers.

”This is Daniel Hallstrom,” I explained. “He makes movies.”

Carlotto grunted. ”Movies? Never heard of him.”

”You must have seen at least a few of my films,” blurted Hallstrom. ”The Russian Affair, Lethal Agent, Heart and Pearls…”

Carlotto did not show any recognition and turned his gaze to the bold, muscular man.

”My name is Rocco,” the man said without having to be asked. ”I am Valeria Bianchi’s driver…and security when needed.”

”So, where have you been?” Carlotto snarled. ”Signora Bianchi is reported kidnapped!”

”Kidnapped?” Rocco repeated without changing his stern face.

Hallstrom fell into a state of shocked silence. ”My production cannot continue without her…” he whispered.

”Luigi,” Tilda began, her voice barely audible. ”Who could have done this? And why?”

”Right now, we can’t say for sure,” I admitted, my mind racing with possibilities as I tried to put together the few pieces I had. ”But I promise you, Tilda — whoever is behind this, they won’t get away with it.”

Rocco stood silent, a sentinel by the door, while

Daniel's gaze flickered from me to Carlotto with casual interest before settling on Tilda. It was clear from his demeanor, the subtle yet unmistakable air of control, that he was accustomed to commanding scenes far more complex than the one unfolding in this suite.

My determination to find Valeria and get to the bottom of this mess burned within me like a raging inferno, fueled by a desire for truth that was as fierce as it was unyielding. Yet even as I vowed to bring her captors to their knees, a chilling thought began to take root in my mind.

The shrill signal of Carlotto's cell interrupted my thoughts.

He listened and looked up at us. "They may have found her."

3

Less than five minutes later, Tilda and I stepped out of Carlotto's car and followed him to a nondescript black sedan, its windows tinted like the eyes of a predator lurking in the shadows. Pounding sounds came from the trunk, and we stood in silent apprehension as a policeman wrenched open the trunk.

It creaked open like the heavy lid of a sarcophagus, revealing its grim treasure. There she lay, bound and gagged, her once-immaculate appearance reduced to a tattered mess. Her eyes, usually vibrant and full of life, now shimmered with tears and fear. The sense of urgency tightened around my chest as I reached in to free her from her restraints.

"Valeria, hold on. I'm here," I whispered, trying to offer some comfort amidst the chaos.

Her disheveled hair clung to her sweat-soaked skin, a stark contrast to her usual glamorous persona. Her wrists bore angry red marks from the ropes that had held her captive, while her once-pristine white dress now hung off her body like the torn shroud of a ghost. She looked up at me, her gaze a mixture of relief and trepidation.

"Luigi, thank God," she breathed as I pulled her out of the trunk and into my arms. I could feel her shivering against me, clinging to me like a lifeline.

Carlotto and Tilda hovered nearby, their faces

etched with concern. Valeria seemed hesitant towards them, her fear not yet dissolved.

"Are you hurt?" I asked, studying her face for signs of injury.

"Nothing serious, but I've never been so scared in my life," she admitted, her trembling hands gripping the fabric of my jacket as if it were the only thing tethering her to reality.

Carlotto eyed the scene with narrowed eyes. "She needs a doctor."

Valeria shook her head and whispered something I could not hear. Then, a black Maserati Quattroporte stopped nearby, and Rocco stepped out, opening the backdoor for her.

"Let's get you out of here," I said, leading her towards Rocco and the Maserati. The soft leather was soothing on our skin, but it couldn't quench the fire that burned inside me – the need to bring justice to the one responsible for this nightmare.

As we rode away from the scene, Valeria's arms wrapped tightly around my waist, I vowed to uncover every hidden clue and end this sordid affair. The question remained – who was behind this twisted scheme?

"Valeria, I need you to tell me everything you remember about what happened before you ended up in the trunk," I urged my mind racing with possibilities.

She hesitated, her gaze flickering between me and the darkened landscape beyond. "It's all a blur, Luigi… I remember arguing with Tilda, and then everything went black."

"Arguing with Tilda?" I echoed a cold suspicion settling in my gut. "About what?"

"Something about money and Carter… but I can't recall the details," Valeria admitted, her brow furrowed with frustration.

My thoughts swirled like a tempest, each piece of information subtly shifting the puzzle before me. Had Tilda been in the beach house as I was struck down? I know she'd been there to wake me up, but I had a feeling the true perpetrator remained shrouded in shadows. I had to bring those shadows into the light.

"Listen, Valeria," I said, my hand finding hers in a gesture of reassurance. "You're safe now, and I promise I'll get to the bottom of this. We'll find out who did this to you, and they'll pay for what they've done."

A tear slipped down her cheek, but she nodded, determination sparking in her eyes. "Grazie, Luigi. I trust you."

Valeria leaned against me, her body trembling with residual fear and exhaustion as I followed her up to her hotel suite.

"Rest now," I murmured, my gaze scanning the empty suite. "I'll keep watch until the others arrive. When morning comes, we'll start anew."

She gave me a quick hug and hesitantly withdrew to the bedroom. I closed the door behind her and sat down, contemplating the last day's events. One: Tilda Larsson called me to Valeria's beach house. Two: I saw Valeria Bianchi shoot her alleged blackmailer, Franco Carter. Three: Valeria asks me to make the killing disappear and refuses to contact the police. Four: I was struck down by some unknown figure. Five: I wake up to the lovely appearance of Signorina Larsson, who tells me Valeria has been kidnapped. Six: Valeria is found, bound and gagged, in the trunk of a car.

The events echoed through my thoughts, each repetition fueling my determination to uncover the secrets hidden beneath the surface of this twisted case.

There was a knock on the door, and Commissario Carlotto came in. His eyes like daggers, he immediately turned to me and commanded sternly:

"Signor Ferro," he said, his voice brimming with intensity, "tell me everything you know about the kidnapping."

"I don't know much more than you do, Commissario," I replied.

"So, why are you here? Why are you working with Signora Bianchi?"

"Officially, I'm not."

"And unofficially?"

"Not even that. I was called to her beach villa last night; she had something she wanted to discuss."

"And what was that?"

"That is private, but as we were talking, someone attacked me, knocked me out cold, and when I was woken up by Signorina Larsson, she told me Valeria had been kidnapped."

"So, someone knocked you out and kidnapped Signora Bianchi at her beach house?"

"As far as I know," I said.

"I don't believe you, Ferro."

The air was thick with tension as I sat on the edge

of a luxurious velvet armchair in Valeria's opulent hotel suite. Despite the grandeur surrounding me, I could only focus on Carlotto's piercing gaze and pressing inquiry.

"Ferro, are you telling me you know nothing more about the kidnapping?" Carlotto asked, his voice sharp and demanding.

I decided not to give him the satisfaction of exposing Valeria, instead opting for the bare minimum truth. "Well, Commissario, as far as I can tell, it was what happened."

Carlotto leaned in closer, his face mere inches from mine. "Do not play games with me, Ferro. I have a feeling there is more to this case than meets the eye, and I need your full cooperation."

My mind raced, struggling to maintain my composure while protecting Valeria. I had to be careful with each word, never revealing too much.

"Commissario, I assure you, I am doing everything in my power to get to the bottom of this. But we cannot jump to conclusions without concrete evidence."

Just then, the door swung open, and in stormed Daniel Hallstrom, his face flushed with frustration.

"Where is she?" he demanded.

"Valeria is resting," I said, indicating the closed bedroom door. "I think it's best that she gets all the rest she can get."

"I cannot believe this! Not only are we behind schedule, but now I have the police and a meddling private investigator breathing down our necks. This film means everything to me...and to Signora Bianchi."

That reminded me that Daniel Hallstrom had had a string of flops over the past decade. Maybe this was his last chance for renewed success.

He turned to Carlotto, his voice seething with anger. "I insist that you and Ferro leave us alone. We have a movie to make!"

Carlotto seemed unmoved by Hallstrom's outburst, his eyes remaining fixed on mine. "We will leave when we are satisfied with the information we have gathered," he replied coolly.

"Fine!" Hallstrom spat, throwing his hands up in exasperation. "But don't come crying to me when your investigation ends up costing us millions!"

"A kidnapping is not something we take lightly," Carlotto said, shifting his gaze to the upset director. "It is a big deal, even in Italy."

I noticed a glint of something in Hallstrom's eyes before he stormed out of the suite, leaving behind an air of bitter resentment.

As the door slammed shut, I couldn't help but feel a sense of relief.

Just as one left, another arrived. Valeria's driver, Rocco, stepped in without knocking. He did not greet us or utter a single word; he just placed himself inside the door.

"She is resting," I said with a nod towards the bedroom door. His stone face did not reveal a single thought or emotion. Did he feel at all, I wondered.

Carlotto turned his gaze to the driver, asking him to take a seat.

"What do you know about the kidnapping?" he started.

"Nothing, Commissario," his expression was stone cold.

"Do you need me more right now, Commissario?" I cut in. "I need a shower and a change. Tell Signora Bianchi I will come tomorrow."

I relaxed a bit as I left the hotel behind me. At least for now, Valeria's secret was safe with me. But how long could I keep this charade going? And at what cost?

*

The sun dipped low behind the ancient walls of San Marino, casting long shadows across the cobbled streets as I approached my apartment building.

"Signor Ferro," said a sultry voice behind me. I turned to see Tilda Larsson approaching, her slender legs emerging from her tight-fitting dress with each deliberate step.

"What are you doing here?" I asked.

"I am worried about Signora Bianchi and thought I could be of assistance."

"Maybe you can," I replied, my lips curling into a half-smile. "But first, let's talk about you."

"Me?" she said innocently, her blue eyes wide with feigned surprise. "What is there to know?"

I wanted to ask if those gracious legs were dressed in stockings or pantyhose, but I stopped myself as I knew it was not considered appropriate to ask such intimate questions.

"Plenty," I murmured instead, my gaze lingering on

her luscious pout. "For instance, how did you get the job as Valeria's personal assistant? And what do you know about this blackmail scheme?"

"Luigi," she sighed, her breath warm against my neck. "You're always looking for the dark side of things, aren't you?"

"Occupational hazard," I replied, my hand brushing hers as I changed direction and headed towards the local taverna. "Come join me for a glass of wine and tell me about it."

"Ah, but we all have our secrets, don't we?" she whispered, following closely behind me. "Some more dangerous than others."

"True," I conceded, my pulse quickening at the thought of unearthing the truth. "But I intend to uncover them all, one way or another."

"Such determination," she purred, her breath now tickling my ear. "I find it quite... exhilarating."

"Careful, Tilda," I warned her, my voice low and controlled. "You wouldn't want to get too close to the fire, would you?"

"Who says I'm afraid of getting burned?" she retorted, her eyes smoldering as we reached the small taverna.

Fabio, the taverna's owner, greeted me warmly and brought us two glasses of Pinot Grigio as we sat down.

"Where do we start?" Tilda asked, clinking my glass, her voice barely a whisper, as if she feared that the darkness might hear her and come to life.

"Every detail counts," I replied, thinking of what had happened and how little I actually knew. "We need to retrace the steps of what's happened. Let's start where you called me last night asking me to go to the beach house."

She leaned in closer and told me a story I was convinced was not the whole truth and even a damn lie. It told of Valeria being worried sick about the blackmailer and how she sought retreat at the beach house. And how she was woken up by an anonymous phone call telling her Signora Bianchi had been kidnapped. She had then driven to the beach villa to see if her boss was there but only found me unconscious in the bed. The rest I knew.

"What do you know about this blackmailing?" I asked.

"Rocco," she said instead of answering. "There's something you should know about him."

"Go on," I prompted, intrigued by this unexpected turn of events.

Tilda hesitated, looking around as if to ensure we weren't being watched. "He's been acting strange lately, ever since this whole blackmail situation began. I've seen him going through Valeria's personal things, making secretive phone calls... I don't know exactly what he's up to, but I don't trust him."

"Interesting," I mused, filing away this information for later. But there was something else, something unspoken between us that made the air thick with desire.

"Tell me, Signorina Larsson, what is your role in all of this?" I asked, leaning closer, my voice low and suggestive. She looked up at me, her lips parting slightly, a faint blush rising in her cheeks.

"I'm just a personal assistant, trying to help my boss," she breathed, her eyes locked on mine, her lips curving into a knowing smile. The game was on.

"Cut the act, Tilda," I growled, taking another sip of the cool wine. "Tell me what you know." The scent of her perfume wafted around me, a heady mix of jasmine and musk that threatened to cloud my judgment.

"Very well," she replied, her voice steady and controlled as she leaned forward over the small table. "But not here. Is your apartment far?"

I placed a ten euro bill on the table and led her away from the taverna. My home was just four doors away. She moved gracefully, her body swaying seductively like the branches of a willow tree caught in a gentle breeze.

My heart raced with anticipation, fueled by the all-consuming desire to learn what Tilda knew about this twisted scheme. The air was thick with tension and something else – a palpable sense of longing that clung to my skin like a lover's touch.

"Signore Ferro," Tilda purred seductively as I opened the door, her eyes sparkling like sapphires in the dim light. "Is this your most private place?"

"At times. Now tell me what you know."

Tilda hesitated for a moment before answering, her fingers playing with the hem of her tight dress.

"I knew about the blackmail," she whispered, her blue eyes clouded with regret. "And I knew about Franco Carter, but I never thought it would go this far. I just gave him Valeria's schedule, nothing more – and I didn't know why he wanted it – he said he was a fan. I know I shouldn't have, but I did…"

"Choices are what define us, Tilda," I said softly, my mind racing with the implications of her confession. "You chose to betray Valeria. And now…"

"Is there nothing I can do to make amends?" she cut in, her voice trembling with emotion as she stepped closer to me. The space between us was charged with an electric current that threatened to ignite at any moment.

"Perhaps," I replied, my resolve wavering as our eyes met and held. "But first, you must prove your loyalty to Valeria – and help me get to the bottom of it all."

"Of course," Tilda murmured, her breath hot against my cheek as she leaned in close. "Whatever it takes."

"Good," I said, my voice barely a whisper as the heat of her body pressed against mine. "Then let's begin."

As our lips met in a searing kiss, fueled by equal parts desire and desperation, I knew that we had crossed a line from which there was no return. With Tilda's help, I would unravel the tangled web of lies and deceit that surrounded us and finally expose the truth about Valeria Bianchi's problems.

And as our passion consumed us, entwining our bodies and souls, I couldn't help but wonder what the future held for us – and whether the price of truth would ultimately be worth the cost.

In the darkness of my bedroom, tangled between sheets and whispered secrets, Tilda and I found solace in each other's arms. My mind raced with questions and doubts, but for now, they were silenced by the heat of our desire.

"Promise me you'll be honest with me," I murmured into Tilda's ear as we lay together, our limbs intertwined like vines on an ancient brick wall.

"For you, for Valeria, and for the truth," she whispered back, sealing our pact with a lingering kiss.

And I did got the answer to my unspoken question: it was stay-up-stockings.

4

The next morning, I awoke to the soft light of dawn filtering through the curtains. Tilda lay beside me, her golden hair tousled and fanned across the pillow like an angel's halo. Her body was a masterpiece in the half-light, and I felt a stirring of desire as my gaze traveled over her curves. But there were more pressing matters to attend to.

"Rise and shine, bella," I murmured, gently nudging her awake. "We have work to do."

Tilda stirred, blue eyes fluttering open as she stretched languidly, her lithe body momentarily on display before she pulled the sheet up to cover herself. A coy smile danced upon her lips – a tantalizing mix of innocence and seduction that made it impossible to resist her allure.

"Buongiorno, Luigi," she purred, her fingers dancing along my forearm. "What's our plan for today?"

Tilda's phone vibrated on the bedside table, jarring her from her interest in me. She glanced at the screen and frowned, concern lining her face.

"There's news coverage about Valeria's kidnapping, and Daniel Hallstrom is quoted about the new film. That doesn't make sense."

"Let me see," I said, taking her phone and scanning the article. Images of Valeria being escorted by me from the trunk of the car accompanied bold headlines, while another picture showed Hallstrom, his trademark grin plastered across his face as he discussed the upcoming movie.

"Something's off," I muttered, handing Tilda back her phone. "Hallstrom shouldn't be using Valeria's misfortune to promote his new film."

"Exactly," Tilda agreed, biting her lip. "What do you think it means?"

"If he's trying to capitalize on the publicity surrounding the kidnapping..." My mind raced with possibilities as I mulled over the implications. "...he may be behind the incident."

Tilda nodded, determination flashing in her eyes. "Let's find the truth, Luigi. Together."

"Agreed," I said, sealing our newfound alliance with a kiss.

My Vespa purred beneath us as we approached the Grand Hotel Rimini, its opulent facade shimmering in the morning sun. Tilda held onto me, her enticing warmth pressed against my back. I sensed a storm brewing within her, a tempest of emotions that threatened to spill over at any moment.

"Are you ready?" I asked, glancing over my shoulder.

"Of course," she replied, her eyes gleaming with determination.

As we entered the hotel, a hushed tension blanketed the lobby like an oppressive fog. The air seemed to tremble with unspoken secrets, and whispers trailed behind us like spectral shadows. It was as though the very walls of the Grand Hotel Rimini had conspired to keep Valeria's enigmatic world hidden from prying eyes.

Valeria was sitting on the terrace, eating breakfast. She looked Tilda up and down, her eyes flicking over her form with disdain. I could feel Tilda stiffen beside me, her body tensing at the silent challenge emanating from Valeria.

"Good morning, Ferro – and Tilda as well," Valeria said, her voice dripping with false sweetness. "I trust you've been... taking good care of each other?"

"Don't be childish, Signora Bianchi," I snapped, unwilling to indulge her taunts. "We need to talk."

"Very well," she sighed, gesturing to the vacant chairs at her table. We sat, and as a waitress approached, we ordered two cappuccinos. Valeria leaned back in her chair, crossing her legs elegantly while regarding Tilda with frosty detachment.

"Tell me, Tilda, have you discovered anything new about my little... predicament?" Valeria inquired, drumming her fingers on the table.

"Actually," Tilda began, her voice trembling ever so slightly, "we think there might be more to this than meets the eye. Have you seen what Hallstrom is saying to the media?"

"Not really." Valeria raised an eyebrow, her lips curling into a sardonic smile. "Do enlighten me."

"Daniel is using your kidnapping to promote the new film," Tilda explained, meeting Valeria's gaze with defiance.

"Interesting," Valeria mused, her eyes narrowing. "And what do you make of that?"

"Find out the truth," I interjected, my jaw set. "We need to know if he's involved in your kidnapping or just capitalizing on it. Either way, we'll get to the bottom of this."

"Very well," Valeria conceded, her gaze shifting back to Tilda. "I'll think about it." She rose from her seat, her every movement deliberate and poised. As she turned to leave, she shot Tilda one last icy glance, leaving no doubt as to the simmering animosity between them.

As the echoes of her footsteps faded away, I looked at Tilda, her cheeks flushed with anger and determination. The game was afoot, and the stakes had never been higher. But with Tilda by my side, I couldn't help but feel that we were on the brink of unraveling the tangled threads of this mystery – and perhaps discovering even more about each other along the way.

Tilda and I had barely finished our coffees before Valeria summoned me to her suite.

The scent of her perfume lingered in the air, a mixture of jasmine and sin. Shivering sensations crawled up my spine as she closed the door behind us, sealing us in that opulent lair.

"Signor Ferro," she purred her voice a velvet caress that ensnared my senses. "I've given your proposal some thought." She moved closer, the rustle of her silk gown a symphony of temptation. "I'm willing to hire you officially to investigate my kidnapping and uncover the truth about Hallstrom."

"Very well," I replied, my voice betraying no hint of the desire her presence sparked within me. "But, we need to agree on the terms."

"Of course." Her smile unfurled with predatory

grace, the deadly allure hidden beneath her exquisite facade now surfacing. "Let's discuss them over something stronger than a cappuccino, shall we?"

As Valeria gracefully prepared two cups of rich, aromatic espresso, the unmistakable danger she exuded became more apparent – a sense of untamed power that was both alluring and disconcerting.

"Firstly," she began, her movements measured and deliberate as she handed me a cup, the steam rising in lazy swirls, "I require your utmost discretion. Everything you learn stays confidential, understood?" Her dark, mesmerizing eyes held mine in a gaze that was as commanding as it was enticing.

"Sure," I agreed, the robust flavor of the espresso blending seamlessly with the faint, intoxicating aroma of her perfume.

"Secondly, I expect daily updates on your progress. And lastly..." Valeria paused, masterfully weaving a thread of tension through the air. "I'll compensate you generously for your services – a proposition you won't easily find elsewhere in Italy."

"Very well," I responded, our cups meeting in a soft clink. The lure of a lucrative payment was tempting, yet the intricacy of the secrets she held, the entangled web she wove, truly captivated me.

"Good," Valeria purred. "If you are quick, you will have time to start with Rocco – my chauffeur – I have to leave for the studio soon."

I found Rocco outside the hotel, leaning against the gleaming Maserati Quattroporte, a cigarette dangling from his lips. His muscular frame tensed as I approached, betraying his unease.

"Bongiorno, Rocco," I said, fixing him with a steely gaze. "I need to ask you some questions about Valeria's kidnapping."

He shifted nervously, avoiding eye contact.

"What do you want to know, Signore?"

"Everything," I replied, searching for any hint of deception in his demeanor. "Start from the beginning."

As Rocco recounted his version of events, I couldn't help but notice how evasive he seemed – as if he were holding something back. I carefully filed away each detail, knowing that those hidden truths would reveal themselves sooner or later. We were getting nowhere but closer to the truth for every lie he told.

"Va bene," I replied, my voice steady despite the pounding of my heart. "So, now tell me what really happened." I let the pistol in my shoulder holster flash visible and decided to lie just as bad as he did. "I heard the police found your fingerprints on the trunk of that car."

"Look, Ferro," he stammered, desperation seeping into his voice. "It wasn't a real kidnapping, alright? She told me to arrange it. Said it would be good for publicity."

"Publicity?" I frowned, feeling the pieces of the puzzle slotting together in my mind. "A dangerous game to play, don't you think?"

"Ask her yourself," Rocco muttered, his eyes downcast. "I just did as I was told."

"And what about your involvement in the blackmailing?"

"Blackmailing?" He scoffed, but I could see the beads of sweat forming on his brow. "You're barking up the wrong tree."

"Franco Carter?" I tried.

"Carter?" He frowned, his bald head shining from sweat. "I think I remember a Carter from a few weeks ago; he was chatting to Signorina Larsson at a party…"

"Really?" I raised an eyebrow, intrigued by this new piece of information. "What were they discussing?"

Rocco hesitated, his eyes darting around the parking lot as if searching for a way to escape my probing questions. "I'm not sure," he finally admitted, his voice barely above a whisper. "But it seemed… intimate."

"Intimate, eh?" The word hung in the air between us, heavy with implications and unspoken desires. "A curious connection indeed."

"But you've been dancing to Valeria's tune all along, haven't you?"

"I just do as I am told. She is my boss…and a big movie star…"

"Of course you do." I patted him roughly on the shoulder, turning to leave. "But remember this, Rocco: the truth has a habit of catching up with those who try to outrun it."

Valeria Bianchi strode down the few steps from the hotel to the parking, looking every bit the movie star she was. Rocco stubbed out his cigarette and opened the backdoor for her to get in.

*

The beach house loomed before me, a pale specter in the afternoon light. It was as if time itself had stopped here, leaving behind a husk that stood as a testament to forgotten sins. I couldn't help but feel a shiver run down my spine as I approached, my footsteps muffled by the damp sand beneath my boots.

"Alright, Carter," I said to myself, my voice barely above a whisper. "Let's see what secrets you've left behind."

The floorboards creaked beneath my feet as I moved through the rooms, my flashlight casting eerie shadows on the wallpaper. The scent of sea salt hung heavy in the air, mingling with the faint, lingering perfume of Valeria's presence. The silence grew thicker with every step, suffocating me in a blanket of dread and anticipation.

"What are you hiding, Valeria?" I murmured to the silence, my fingers tracing the outline of the dresser where I searched yesterday. "What secrets did Carter take to his grave?"

Once again, I looked at the naked blonde in the photo. The young woman was not totally in focus, but there was something familiar with the nose, the cheeks, and the pouting red lips. I pocketed it for the future and returned to the downstairs living room.

As I stepped inside, the room held a suspended stillness, its air thick with the echoes of a night steeped in violence and whispers of a past rapidly unfurling. It was here, in this very spot, where Valeria Bianchi had stood – a figure of tragic elegance, her silhouette etched against the pallor of moonlight that had invaded the room. I positioned myself where she had been, attempting to see the room through her eyes, to feel the weight of her desperation and fear.

The place where Franco Carter's life had ended was chillingly unremarkable now, yet it seemed to pulsate with a silent, grim energy. His body had lain there, motionless and final, a testament to the dire extremes of human actions. My eyes then drifted to the window – to the left. That was the pane that had shattered under the violent kiss of the bullet, its fragments a crystal cascade in the moonlit chaos.

Compelled by a detective's instinct, an unspoken whisper in the depths of my consciousness, I moved towards the window. The frame offered an unobstructed view of the small backyard, its rough driveway cutting through the untamed embrace of nature. There, about five meters beyond, stood a large tree, its branches swaying gently in the breeze from the sea.

A sense of urgency propelled me outside, my steps guided by an unshakable hunch that gnawed at my senses. The tree stood there, an unwitting participant in the night's grim theater. My eyes scanned its bark, searching for a sign, a clue. And there it was – nestled a few centimeters into the bark, almost shy in its concealment, was the bullet.

The discovery sent a shiver down my spine, a chilling affirmation of the grim reality that had unfolded here. The bullet was a silent witness, a bearer of truth in a tale mired in deception and shadows. With its retrieval, a piece of the puzzle lay in my hands, a tangible link to the events that had irrevocably altered the course of several lives, including my own.

A sudden smell of something burning, like a campfire, met my nostrils.

"Looking for something?" a gruff voice shattered the silence.

I spun around, gun drawn, to find myself face-to-face with a scruffy bum – his eyes wild, his clothes tattered, and a wicked grin spreading across his dirt-streaked face.

"Who are you?" I demanded, my finger twitching on the trigger.

"Someone who doesn't like nosy detectives," he spat, lunging at me with surprising speed.

I dodged his first strike, feeling the wind from his fist as it whistled past my ear. But he was relentless, his movements fluid and deadly, like a viper coiled to strike. We danced a deadly waltz, our bodies moving in a violent rhythm that left no room for mercy or hesitation. He reeked of cheap whiskey and anger.

"Valeria sent you, didn't she?" I gasped between blows, trying to piece together the puzzle while fighting for my life.

"No one sends me," he sneered, landing a punch that sent me staggering back. "Maybe I just don't like your face."

"Either way," I growled, regaining my footing, "you won't stop me from finding the truth."

"First, you'll have to get through me," he replied, lunging forward once more.

We continued our dance of death, the taste of blood

and sweat on my lips, the sound of our grunts and curses filling the air like a symphony of violence. And as I fought against this stranger, this ghost from a past I had yet to uncover, I couldn't help but feel that something far darker than desire or ambition lay at the heart of this tangled web.

"Even if you kill me," I hissed, dodging another blow, "someone else will come looking. Secrets don't stay buried forever."

"Then they'll meet the same fate as you," he snarled, his eyes burning with a ferocity that both terrified and intrigued me.

"Fine," I spat, gritting my teeth as I prepared for one final, desperate gambit. "But just remember – you can't outrun the past forever."

"Doesn't matter," he snarled, lunging forward with an unexpected ferocity that caught me off guard.

His fists connected with my jaw, sending a shockwave of pain coursing through my skull. My vision blurred momentarily, but I forced myself back onto my feet, my determination to unravel this twisted mystery only growing stronger.

"Someone sent you to kill me," I said, wiping the blood from my lips. "Who was it? Rocco?"

He laughed, cold and bitter. "You think you're so clever, don't you, detective? But you're out of your depth here."

"Am I?" I shot back, my voice laced with contempt. "It seems to me you're nothing more than a hired thug, a pawn in someone else's game."

"Believe what you want," he replied, feigning

disinterest. "But when I'm done with you, there'll be nothing left but a broken man begging for mercy."

"You think you are a good fighter, don't you?" I taunted, dodging his next blow with calculated precision. "But you underestimate me, amico."

"Amico?" he sneered. "We are not friends."

"True," I conceded, landing a punch to his gut that left him reeling. "But we could have been allies."

"Never," he growled, rallying his strength for another attack. "I have no use for men like you."

"Men like me?" I asked, raising an eyebrow. "You mean men who seek the truth, who fight against the corruption and greed that festers in the shadows?"

"Your arrogance is astounding," he replied, his eyes narrowing to dangerous slits. "But it won't save you."

"Perhaps not," I admitted, my heart pounding in my chest as we clashed once more, our bodies locked in a desperate struggle for control. "But at least I'll die knowing I tried to do what was right."

"Right?" he laughed, delivering a powerful blow that sent me sprawling to the floor. "There is no right or wrong here, detective – only power and those willing to do whatever it takes to wield it."

"Then I pity you," I whispered, the darkness closing in as consciousness threatened to slip away. "For a life without honor is no life at all."

"Save your pity for yourself," he spat, his boot connecting with my temple as the world around me faded to black.

5

The salty breeze rustled the leaves of the palm trees as I leaned against the wall of the beach villa, clutching my side where a wound throbbed with each heartbeat. The waves crashed onto the shore, interspersed with the distant cries of seagulls. My thoughts spinning, trying to make sense of the tangled web I had found myself in.

"Luigi!" Tilda's voice cut through the air like a sharpened blade, her Swedish accent tinged with concern. She appeared from the shadows, an ethereal vision in her flowing white dress that clung to her every curve. Her blue eyes bore into mine, wide with surprise and worry.

"What has happened to you?" she asked, her hands cupping my face as she examined me.

"Nothing I can't handle," I grumbled, attempting to downplay my injury. Her touch sent shivers down my spine, stirring a familiar cocktail of desire and trepidation.

"Please, let me help you." Her concern was genuine, or so it seemed. In this shadowy realm of lies and deceit, who could truly say what lay hidden behind those beguiling eyes?

Her slender arm wrapped around my waist, offering support as I hobbled inside the villa. We moved slowly, each step an exercise in restraint as we navigated the treacherous path towards the villa. Her touch, though gentle, sent shivers down my spine.

"Valeria will not be pleased to see you like this," she murmured as we crossed the threshold, her breath warm against my ear. I fought the urge to lean into her, to lose myself in the comfort she offered. But there were more pressing matters at hand.

"Let her worry about her own secrets," I replied curtly, my resolve strengthened by the memory of the man's hard and skillful punches. "I have my own demons to face."

"Luigi, you must know how dangerous this all is," Tilda whispered, her voice quivering with fear as she eased me onto a plush velvet chaise. "Why do you persist?"

"Because I cannot simply walk away," I confessed, my eyes locked on hers, searching for any hint of duplicity. "Not when there are still answers to be found, people to protect."

"Even if it costs you everything?" Her eyes filled with unshed tears, the weight of her question hanging heavy between us.

"Especially then," I replied, my voice barely audible above the distant crashing of the waves. For in that moment, I knew I would sacrifice everything to unravel this tangled web. Even if it meant losing myself to the allure of the one woman whose touch could bring me both salvation and damnation.

The afternoon sun flickered against Tilda's face, casting her delicate features into sharp relief. Her eyes, a stormy blue, bore into mine as if trying to divine my thoughts. I swallowed hard, feeling the pain from my injuries throb in time with my racing heart.

"Tell me, Tilda," I began, my voice steady despite the simmering suspicion gnawing at the edges of my consciousness. "What brought you here tonight? What is your role in all this?"

She hesitated for a moment, and I could see the wheels turning behind her eyes, calculating her response. "I'm just Valeria's assistant, Luigi."

"Is that truly all there is?" I pressed, refusing to let her sidestep my questions so easily. The air between us grew heavy with tension, an electric current threatening to ignite at any moment.

"Perhaps," she replied cryptically, a coy smile playing at the corners of her mouth. She moved closer, her fingers trailing along the curve of my jaw. My breath hitched, caught in the snare of her touch. "Perhaps not."

Her proximity was intoxicating, the scent of her perfume a heady blend of jasmine and temptation. It took every ounce of willpower I possessed to keep my thoughts focused on the task at hand. But Tilda was a clever adversary, and she knew exactly how to wield her allure like a weapon.

"Signorina Larsson," I murmured, struggling to remain detached even as her fingers traced the outline of my collarbone. "You must realize that my investigation will lead me to the truth, one way or another."

"Then perhaps," she whispered, her lips hovering tantalizingly close to my ear, "you should focus less on what you think you know and more on what you desire." Her breath was warm against my skin, raising goosebumps along the nape of my neck as her words wrapped around me like a lover's embrace.

"Desire can be a dangerous thing," I warned, my voice hoarse with need. The weight of her gaze held me captive, and for a fleeting moment, I allowed myself to be ensnared by it. "Especially when it clouds one's judgment."

"Ah, but Luigi," Tilda countered, her fingers playing idly with the buttons of my shirt, each subtle touch sending shivers through my body. "Isn't that what makes it so exhilarating?"

The air in the room grew thick with unspoken desires, the heat of our bodies drawing us closer and closer together. My resolve wavered, the lines between temptation and duty blurring until they were almost indistinguishable.

"Perhaps," I conceded, my voice barely audible over the pounding of my heart. "But some mysteries are better left unsolved."

"Then let us leave them be," Tilda murmured, sealing our fates with a searing kiss that threatened to consume us both.

*

Beneath the dim glow of the lamplight, Tilda's body was an exquisite sculpture of feminine allure. Her long, smooth legs wrapped around me like tendrils of an irresistible siren, drawing me in with a grip that left no room for escape. My hands traced the curve of her round bum, fingers sinking into the supple flesh as I marveled at its perfect symmetry. She arched her back, pushing her tight waist and pert breasts against my chest, our breaths mingling in the charged air between us. Her face, framed by golden strands of hair, held an expression of pure seduction, those sapphire eyes promising heaven and hell in equal measure.

"Tell me, Luigi" she whispered, her voice sultry and honeyed. "Tell me what you need."

"You," I managed, my voice choked with desire. "I need you."

"Then have me," she murmured, guiding me to her with a firm hand and deliberate intent.

The passion ignited between us was a wildfire consuming everything in its path. The investigation, my suspicions – all were momentarily sidelined as we lost ourselves in each other. Our bodies moved in sync, a dance as old as time itself, yet fresh and thrilling in the heat of our connection.

As the fire burned down to embers, we lay entwined amidst sweat-dampened sheets, the silence of the night heavy around us. In that moment, I should have felt nothing but satiation and contentment. Instead, doubt crept in, like a serpent slithering through the grass, insinuating itself into my thoughts.

"Who are you really?" I asked, unable to push the question from my mind.

"Not important," Tilda replied, her fingers tracing lazy circles on my chest. "Tonight, we were just two people finding solace in one another's arms."

"Solace?" I echoed, my heart heavy with the weight of a thousand unasked questions. "Or distraction?"

"Does it matter?" She tilted her head up to gaze into my eyes, a ghost of a smile playing on her lips.

"Maybe not tonight," I conceded, pulling her closer and seeking warmth in our embrace. "But other days will come."

"Si," she agreed, nestling her head against my shoulder. "Tomorrow is another day."

As sleep claimed us both, I couldn't shake the nagging sense that I was being manipulated by this enigmatic woman. Her body had been an irresistible temptation, but beneath that seductive exterior lay secrets I had yet to uncover. And as the evening surrendered to the encroaching twilight, I vowed to peel back the layers of deception and mystery, no matter what the cost.

The sun had sunk below the horizon, leaving only traces of its warmth in the air. Shadows stretched across the villa, and the beach beyond was shrouded in the dark veil of night. I glanced at my wrist watch, just eight. Tilda, with her mysterious ways, was sound asleep beside me, her breaths deep and even, oblivious to the world around her.

Quietly, I slid out of bed, careful not to disturb her peaceful slumber. The room was dimly lit by the moonlight filtering through the curtains, casting a silver glow on Tilda's serene face. I stepped towards the window, gazing out at the expansive darkness, my thoughts clouded with the complexities of the case.

In the silence, my mind replayed the whispers of blackmail, echoing in the stillness. I murmured to myself, pondering over the words and their implications, when suddenly, Tilda stirred in her sleep. I turned to look at her, but she remained in the grips of her dreams, unaware of the secrets that lurked in the shadows.

"Focus on Valeria," I reminded myself, my voice a low whisper in the quiet room. "Don't get lost in the shadows."

But a part of me knew that sometimes, it's the shadows that reveal the most telling truths. With a heavy heart, I turned away from the window, my resolve strengthening. I needed to uncover everything, no matter how perilous the path.

"Be cautious, Luigi," I thought, hearing Tilda's voice in my head as if she were warning me. Some truths, indeed, might be perilous to unearth, but I knew that in the pursuit of justice, no stone could be left unturned.

But the allure of the unknown was too powerful, a siren's call that beckoned me towards the abyss. Armed with nothing but my flashlight and determination, I ventured out into the night, the sand beneath my feet cold and unyielding.

I made my way towards the beach, the soft crunch of sand under my shoes marking my passage through the cool night air. The moon cast a silver glow over the sea, creating a path of light that seemed to lead into infinity. The rhythmic sound of waves lapping against the shore was a soothing counterpoint to the turmoil of thoughts swirling in my head.

As I approached the water's edge, my eyes caught a peculiar sight nestled between two dunes. It was a makeshift abode, cleverly concealed and crafted from driftwood, old tarps, and bits of discarded netting. This was the living quarters of a mysterious vagrant, an enigma in this otherwise tranquil place.

Intrigued, I ventured closer, curiosity piqued. The shelter was ingeniously assembled, hinting at a resident who valued privacy and perhaps had secrets to keep.

Pausing, I surveyed the surroundings, listening for any sign of the inhabitant. The only response was the whisper of the wind and the steady breath of the sea. I decided to investigate further, stepping cautiously towards the shelter, my senses heightened in search of the unknown.

The makeshift shelter was crude, yet it bore the unmistakable marks of someone who had once known order and discipline. My curiosity piqued, I stepped inside and began my investigation, the beam of my flashlight cutting through the darkness like a knife.

The air was heavy with an earthy musk, reminiscent of damp wood, wet sand and burnt wood; a scent that clung to the very essence of this place like a shroud.

"What the devil...," I muttered as my gaze fell upon a worn paycheck amid the scattered debris. It was addressed to one Louis Celotti and was issued by the war veterans foundation, an unmistakable hint at the bum's past. And a probable cause to his fighting skills. My fingers brushed against the crumpled paper.

"Louis Celotti," I whispered to myself, rolling the name around my tongue, tasting its unfamiliarity. "Why are you here?"

But it was not the paycheck that truly captured my attention. No, it was the numerous magazine clippings of Valeria that littered the small space. They were scattered like fallen rose petals, their glossy surfaces reflecting the cold light of my flashlight. A shrine to obsession, a testament to the depths of human desire.

And among those images, like a serpent coiled among the flowers, lay a box of ammunition – gleaming and deadly, a promise of violence yet to come. I swallowed hard, feeling the acidic taste of bile rise in my throat. The pieces of this twisted puzzle were beginning to fall into place, but their edges still eluded me.

"Why are you so obsessed with Valeria?" I asked the empty shelter, knowing no answer would be forthcoming. Yet, as I stood there in that cramped space, surrounded by the detritus of another man's life, I couldn't help but feel a strange kinship with the enigmatic Louis Celotti.

We were both drawn to Valeria, like moths to a flame, captivated by her seductive allure, ensnared by her undeniable power. I shook my head, trying to banish the thoughts of Tilda's lithe body entwined with my own, the taste of her lips still fresh upon mine. But the specter of temptation haunted me still, a ghostly whisper that echoed through my very soul.

"Get a grip of it," I told myself sternly, forcing my mind back to the task at hand. I was no stranger to the seductive dance that played out between men and women, but this was different. This was a game of shadows and secrets, a dangerous waltz where the stakes were higher than ever before.

"I can't afford to be distracted," I vowed as I left the

shelter behind. The moon cast a silvery glow over the beach, like a sensual caress upon the water's edge. The night air was heavy with salt and secrets, wrapping around me as I contemplated the unsettling discoveries within Louis Celotti's makeshift lair.

If Rocco was the one behind the fake kidnapping, maybe this man was the one behind the blackmail. I did not trust anyone or anything they'd told me.

"I will find you, Louis Celotti," I promised into the wind, feeling the weight of my newfound resolve settle like armor around my heart. "And I will bring you to the light."

The darkness held no comfort for me now, only the promise of unanswered questions and hidden truths waiting to be revealed. A warm breeze whispered along my skin, carrying with it the faintest hint of temptation, a siren's song that beckoned me back towards the villa where Tilda awaited.

My mind was a tempest of conflicting emotions – the elusive Louis Celotti, the growing suspicion surrounding Tilda, and the burning desire that still smoldered within me.

"What should I do?" I muttered under my breath, feeling the weight of my dilemma pressing down on my chest like a leaden anchor.

As I entered the bedroom she was awake.

"Luigi," came her voice, a sultry whisper carried on the breeze. "Come here. I am starving..."

"So am I," I replied curtly, shaking my head to rid the images of our passionate encounter that danced in my mind like lascivious flames. "Get dressed. We can get dinner in Rimini if we hurry."

"What are you talking about, darling?" she purred, her fingers brushing against my forearm like the delicate caress of a silk scarf. "I have a hunger for something else..."

"No," I insisted, pulling away from her touch with an effort that left me breathless. "I need energy and we both need to get out of this terrible villa. Clear our minds."

"As you like," she sighed, her disappointment palpable beneath the veil of seduction. She swung her shapely legs over the side of the bed and let her dress slip over her slender shoulder–no underwear needed.

"I'll lead the way on my Vespa and you can follow," I murmured softly, the words tasting bitter on my tongue as I turned my back on her magnetic allure.

A balmy breeze tousled my hair as I parked my Vespa next to Tilda's car. The dim street lights cast a sultry glow on the streets of Rimini. Tilda looked at me with those piercing blue eyes, her golden locks framing her face like a halo, but there was nothing innocent about her. She was the embodiment of temptation, and I was walking right into her trap.

"Let's take one of the restaurants here," I said, leading her across Parco Federico Fellini.

I knew I should have been suspicious, but the way she moved in that form-fitting black dress made it impossible to resist. As we approached a restaurant situated along the park, I could feel the tension between us, thick enough to cut with a knife.

"Buona sera," greeted the waiter as he seated us under the starlit sky, surrounded by the soft murmur of Italian conversations and the clinking of wine glasses. Most tourists had retreated for the night, leaving the place to be savored by a few locals and people like us who basked in the hidden allure of Rimini.

As the waiter presented us with the menu, my senses were teased by the enticing aromas of Italian cuisine wafting from the kitchen.

"I'll let you choose, Luigi," Tilda said flirtatiously, her fingers brushing against mine as she handed me the menu. With each course that arrived - antipasto, pasta and finally, the most succulent osso buco I'd ever tasted

- our conversation grew more intimate, punctuated by sips of ruby-red Chianti.

Across the park, the facade of the Grand Hotel Rimini stood illuminated, its grandiose architecture a silent witness to our charged rendezvous. It was then that I noticed them: a group of youths standing by the street opposite the restaurant. They chatted amongst themselves, laughter bubbling up like champagne, their gazes fixed on Tilda.

"Seems like you have some admirers" I remarked, nodding subtly towards the group. She glanced in their direction, and I could see her demeanor change. Her eyes widened, and her lips pursed – she was trying to hide something, I could feel it.

"Ah, ragazzi" she laughed nervously, "You know how they are, always looking for a pretty face."

It wasn't just a pretty face they were after, though. My instincts told me there was more to the story, but I decided to hold my tongue for now. We finished our meal, our conversation strained under the weight of unspoken secrets. I could tell that behind those seductive blue eyes, Tilda Larsson was hiding something, and I was determined to unravel her mysteries one tangled thread at a time.

"Excuse me for a moment, Tilda. I need to have a word with those ragazzi," I said, rising from my seat.

"Luigi, please, let it be," Tilda's voice was tinged with a hint of desperation, but I was already striding towards the youths, my investigator's instinct overriding her plea.

"Buonasera, ragazzi," I greeted the youths, adopting

a casual tone. "I couldn't help but notice you were admiring my dinner companion."

The youths exchanged wary glances, their initial enthusiasm dampening under my scrutinizing gaze.

"Blondie Swede!" one finally blurted, his attempt at nonchalance failing miserably.

"Scusa?" I feigned ignorance, my brow creasing. "Who's this Blondie Swede?"

"You don't know?" another youth asked, skepticism lacing his voice. "She's a famous porn actress!"

I saw the hesitation in their eyes, a reluctance to share more. Leaning in, I adopted a more persuasive tone, "Come on, ragazzi, I'm just a curious soul. Show me."

There was a moment of hesitation before the third youth, egged on by his friends' nods, handed me his phone. The images and videos that flickered across the screen were more than mere confirmation. Tilda Larsson, or "Blondie Swede" as they knew her, was unmistakable–it was the girl on the photo in my pocket. Each click on the guy's phone revealed more of her secret life, culminating in a video clip with a title that sent a chill down my spine: 'Producer Franco Carter.'

My heart raced, an odd mix of excitement and betrayal coursing through my veins.

"Thank you, ragazzi," I muttered, handing back the phone. I returned to the table, trying to maintain my composure in front of Tilda. Our eyes met, and I could see the fear flickering behind her icy blues.

"Is there something you'd like to tell me, Tilda?" I asked, my voice low and dangerous.

"Luigi, please understand," she stammered, her words laced with desperation. "It's not who I am anymore. I did what I had to do to survive."

"Survive? By selling your body for the pleasure of others?" I retorted, my anger boiling over.

"Luigi, I had no choice," she pleaded, tears welling in her eyes. "I needed the money to take care of my sick mother. Carter took advantage of me, and he tried to destroy Valeria too."

"Valeria?" I whispered, the pieces of the puzzle falling into place. Tilda nodded, her voice cracking as she told me how Franco Carter had filmed an unreleased test video with Valeria.

As the truth unraveled before me, I felt a storm of conflicting emotions: betrayal, sympathy, and a burning desire to uncover the depths of this sordid tale.

The taste of betrayal clung to the air like an unwanted perfume, its oppressive scent lingering between Tilda and me. I stood there, my gaze locked onto her, as the echoes of laughter from the youths across the street still rang in my ears. The park's shadows played tricks on my mind, but I could not ignore the stark truth before me.

"Luigi, please," Tilda whispered, her voice trembling with unspoken secrets. "It's not what you think."

"What am I supposed to think, Tilda?" I replied, my words laced with a bitter venom I had never thought I'd use with her. "You're the very same girl from the photo in Valeria's dresser, and now I find out you've been starring in Franco Carter's films?"

"Is that what those ragazzi told you?" she cried, her

eyes glistening with tears that threatened to spill over. "I had no choice, Luigi. I was young, desperate, and he... he preyed upon me."

"Preyed?" I scoffed, struggling to contain the anger bubbling beneath my skin. "Tilda, you were his star – 'Blondie Swede,' wasn't it? It seems to me like you two shared more than just a professional relationship."

Her face crumpled at my words, and for a moment, I glimpsed the vulnerability hidden beneath her seductive facade.

"He took advantage of my desperation," she admitted, her voice barely audible. "But I'm not that person anymore, Luigi. I swear."

As I stared into her pleading eyes, I couldn't help but recall the vibrant colors of Rimini's ancient frescoes – once vivid, now faded, but somehow still imbued with all their original intensity. Was it possible that Tilda, too, had been transformed by time and circumstance?

"Tell me about Carter," I demanded, my voice a low growl. "What was his role to all this?"

"Franco... he's a monster," she answered, her voice cracking with the weight of her memories. "He lured me in with promises of fame and fortune, only to destroy my life for his own sick pleasure."

"Go on," I urged, my heart tightening at the pain etched across her delicate features.

"Valeria, too, was one of his victims," Tilda revealed, the words spilling out like water from a broken dam. "She never wanted anyone to know about her past. She was desperate to keep it buried."

"Yes," I urged, my gaze never leaving hers.

"Valeria did a test film years ago, before her fame," she confessed, tears shimmering in her eyes. "Carter kept it hidden, threatening to release it if she didn't pay him off."

"Merda," I muttered under my breath. I could see the shame etched upon Tilda's face, the weight of her secret bearing down on her like an ancient, crumbling fresco.

"Valeria paid Carter for years," Tilda continued, her voice barely audible. "She thought she had finally escaped him when he disappeared, but after his bankruptcy he came back, demanding even more money."

"Then this unreleased film is the key to stop this blackmail," I said, determination surging through me like a jolt of espresso. "If we can find it, we can put an end to this once and for all."

As the implications settled upon me like a cloak of shadows, I felt a chill creep down my spine. The truth was more twisted than I could have imagined, casting its dark tendrils over everyone involved.

"Where does this leave us, Tilda?" I asked, the weight of my dilemma heavy upon my shoulders. "Can I trust you?"

"Luigi, you can trust me," she whispered, her eyes brimming with sincerity. "I swear, I've left that life behind. All I want now is to put this behind me."

"Alright, Tilda, we're in this together," I said, my voice firm with determination. "But we need a plan."

"Agreed," she nodded, her eyes shining with renewed hope.

"First things first, we need to get our hands on that test film of Valeria. It's the key to putting an end to this blackmail scheme," I explained, my mind racing through the possible scenarios.

"Unfortunately, I don't know where he kept it," Tilda admitted, her brows furrowing with concern.

"Then we'll have to find out," I ascertained.

"Thank you, Luigi. For everything," she whispered, her fingers intertwining with mine.

"Enough of the pleasantries, cara mia," I said, a ghost of a smile playing on my lips. "We have work to do."

We walked over to the hotel and found solace in Tilda's spacious room.

As we sat there, plotting our course of action beneath the silken veil of night, I couldn't help but feel an odd mixture of desire and loyalty. The tangled threads of Tilda's past had ensnared me in a web of temptation, yet her vulnerability and strength had also ignited within me a fierce urge to protect her.

In the hours that followed, we discussed tirelessly to unravel the secrets surrounding Franco Carter and his sordid scheme.

"How much did you really know about Carter's blackmail?" I questioned, my mind racing with possibilities. I could feel the electrifying mix of intrigue and danger coursing through my veins, awakening something primal within me.

"Luigi, you must understand," Tilda implored, her voice laced with vulnerability. "I never meant to hurt you or Valeria. Carter forced me into this dark world, exploiting my weakness, manipulating me until I was but a puppet on his twisted stage." She stepped closer, the heat radiating from her body caressing my senses like a forbidden temptation. "But we have the power to break free, to end this nightmare once and for all."

"Can we really, Tilda?" I questioned, my gaze locked with hers, searching for the truth that lay hidden behind her seductive facade. "But, with the blackmailer murdered and you an innocent bystander, who killed Franco Carter, where is the test film and who is continuing the blackmail scheme?"

Tilda nodded, her despair momentarily replaced by a flicker of hope. "We have to find it? The most probable culprits is either Rocco or that man on the beach."

"Yeah, Louis Celotti. I have to talk to him."

"Valeria trust you," Tilda whispered, her azure eyes pleading with me. "Please, Luigi, help her. Help us both."

The air around us seemed to crackle with energy as we sat there, our fingers entwined, the weight of our shared secrets pressing down upon us like a stifling shroud. Yet beneath the cloak of darkness, a glimmer of hope shone through – a beacon of light guiding us towards justice and perhaps, in time, even trust.

The rising sun cast a warm glow on Tilda's face, her golden hair haloed by its rays. She looked like an angel, but I knew better now. Her beauty had lured me in, ensnaring me in a web of deceit and desire. The fountain in Parco Federico Fellini rippled softly from the open balcony door, oblivious to the tempest raging within my heart.

"I'll go back to the beach," I stated, trying to sound more certain than I felt. "Before we can come further in this we need to talk to Celotti."

I knew that one thing was certain: the path to redemption would be paved with both desire and danger. I couldn't bear looking into her eyes, bright blue pools that reflected both innocence and guile. My hand clenched involuntarily, the damning evidence against her burning a hole through my pocket. Those photos and videos—proof of her past and connection to Franco Carter—the man who had turned Valeria Bianchi's life into a living hell. And yet, as I stood there, torn between duty and desire, I couldn't bring myself to distrust her.

7

I returned to the beach shack where Louis Celotti, the homeless war veteran, resided. The sun stood just over the eastern horizon, casting a golden glow upon the sand and waves. Yet, despite the serene surroundings, a storm brewed within me – my heart hammered against my ribs as if trying to escape the cage of betrayal.

I parked my Vespa a safe distance from the shack, remaining concealed behind an abandoned fishing boat. My investigator instincts were on high alert, every sense sharpened by the lingering taste of Tilda's deceit.

I walked slowly and with care towards the makeshift home, knowing that this was the loose end I needed to tie up before I could close this case.

Still, I couldn't shake off the nagging feeling that something was amiss. The air seemed to hum with unspoken tension as if even the seagulls perched atop the shack knew more than they let on.

I found a place behind some dry shrubbery where I could hide and survey the place. As I peered through a pair of binoculars, the humble structure came into focus, its wooden planks weathered by salt and time. I scanned the area, searching for any signs of life or movement.

It was quiet and silent. Just the sound of the wind whipping through the tall grass that surrounded the shack and the distant lapping of the waves. A shiver ran down my spine, and not just from the cool breeze that teased the hairs on the back of my neck.

"Damn it, Louis," I whispered, frustration simmering beneath my skin. "Where are you? What do you know?"

I continued to observe from afar, my eyes glued to the shack like a hawk searching for prey. A search fueled by desire, temptation, and power. Little did I know that the secrets hidden within that ramshackle abode would soon send my world crashing down in a tangled web of lies and deceit.

"This is no sprint," I murmured to myself, gripping the binoculars tighter. "When doing a stakeout, always be prepared for a marathon."

And so, I waited, my senses straining for any indication that the answers I sought were within reach. The sun climbed higher in the sky, casting its light upon the shadowy world I had come to inhabit, illuminating the path that lay ahead – a path paved with danger, deception, and, ultimately, the truth.

And then, like a specter materializing from the depths of my darkest fears, a figure appeared. His hulking frame cast an ominous shadow as he approached the shack with a purposeful stride, his eyes locked on his destination. My heart slammed against my ribcage, and an icy sweat prickled my brow.

What was Rocco, Valeria's burly driver, doing here?

I tensed as he reached the shack, and instinctively, I knew what was about to happen, but I was powerless to stop it.

"Louis!" Rocco barked, his voice echoing across the desolate beach.

The bundle of blankets and debris stirred, revealing the disheveled figure of Louis Celotti, war veteran and Valeria's ardent admirer. He looked confused, alarmed, and vulnerable – the perfect prey for a predator like Rocco.

"What is this about?" Louis demanded, his voice trembling with fear.

"This," Rocco replied coldly.

Without another word, he pulled out a gun from his jacket and fired. The sound of the gunshot ripped through the air like a thunderclap, shattering the fragile silence that had settled over the scene.

"No!" I cried out, the roar of the gunshot reverberating in my ears.

But it was too late. Louis's body crumpled to the ground like a discarded ragdoll, his life snuffed out in an instant. Blood seeped into the sands below, staining them a dark crimson, and my world tilted on its axis.

"Why, Rocco?" I cursed under my breath, my hands shaking with a mixture of shock, fury, and helplessness.

The scent of gunpowder spread in the wind, a bitter perfume that belied its deadly purpose. Rocco's brutish form loomed over Celotti's lifeless body, his expression cold, calculating – devoid of any semblance of humanity. The sour taste of bile and betrayal stung my throat as I watched, hidden from view, my heart thundering like a caged beast.

Rocco ruffled through the debris around the lifeless form, eventually finding what he was after, revealing a sleek rifle, which he carefully placed beside Celotti's body, forging a grotesque scene of self-defense.

Rocco nodded, admiring his handiwork. This man, this monster, reveled in the art of deception, painting a false narrative with the same meticulous care one would lavish upon a Renaissance masterpiece.

"Rest in peace, you fool," he spat, kicking sand over the bloodied corpse. A cruel smile crept across Rocco's face as he turned on his heel, making a hasty exit from the scene of his crime.

Cloaked by the velvety darkness, I stepped out from my hiding place, my heart heavy with the burden of truth. Tonight, the shadows would be my confidante, bearing witness to the sordid secrets hidden beneath the glamor and decadence of Italian high society. And as I slowly approached the shack, I made a promise to the man who had paid the ultimate price for his devotion to a movie star.

"I'm sorry, Louis," I thought despairingly, my resolve wavering like the flames of a dying candle. "Forgive me for my inaction."

I fished up my cell phone and dialed.

*

As the sun reached its zenith, brightening the world, I knew that the time for secrets was over. Red and white tape with the words "Polizia Municipale" waved in the breeze, marking the crime scene. Investigators and technicians were all over the scene, but it was up to me to untangle this twisted web of seduction, power, and deceit.

"Ferro!" a familiar voice called out. Commissario Carlotto stepped toward me from the shack, his impeccably tailored suit a stark contrast to the rough beach surrounding him.

"Carlotto," I replied tersely, my eyes narrowing in suspicion. "Am I free to go?"

"That depends," he said, his dark eyes searching mine for a flicker of trust. "But, I know where to find you. You can trust me."

"I trust you, but only as far as I can throw you," I replied cautiously, the words heavy with the weight of unspoken doubts.

Carlotto's lips curled into a wry smile.

"That is more than enough for now," he conceded. "If you know what's behind this, you must cooperate and bring those responsible to justice."

"Sure," I nodded, my determination hardening like steel forged in the fires of passion and betrayal. "But I also have an obligation to my client."

"Is that the client who was kidnapped?"

I nodded. "I'll get back to you soon, Commissario."

He extended a hand in alliance. As our fingers clasped together, I felt a surge of inner strength coursing through me, bolstering my resolve for the challenges that lay ahead.

"For truth," I whispered, my voice resolute as we shook hands, sealing our pact.

"For justice," Carlotto replied, and I left the beach.

An hour later, I sat alone at a beach bar, surrounded by tourists with red skin, searching for relief from the scorching sun. Families speaking German, Spanish,

French, and, of course, English. A bottle of iced beer idled in my hand, and my mind spun through the labyrinth of the case that had consumed me. It felt like a Gordian knot, each thread interwoven with lies, deceit, and hidden motives. The more I unraveled, the more complex it became.

At the heart of it all was the enigmatic Valeria Bianchi. She was like a sphinx, her motives as cryptic as her actions. She had shot Franco Carter, but was it truly self-defense, as she claimed? Carter had been blackmailing her with a pornographic test film, a secret so potent it could obliterate her career. Killing him might have been her only way out. Yet, why would she then order her own kidnapping?

That's where Rocco came in. Rocco, the loyal brute, who admitted to staging Valeria's kidnapping on her orders. Was it a desperate ploy to deflect suspicion or part of a more intricate plan? And then there was Louis, the ex-soldier, living rough on the beach. He had struck me down, yet his motives remained a mystery. He was a fan of Valeria, obsessed to the point of madness, but how deep did his fanaticism run? Was he just a pawn in Valeria's game, or did he have his own agenda?

Rocco had killed Louis, a clean-up job, perhaps? But why kill Louis if he was merely an obsessed fan? Unless Louis knew something crucial, something that threatened to expose the entire charade.

I swirled the bottle in my hand, watching it catch the light. It dawned on me, then, the possible solution to this intricate puzzle. What if all these events were orchestrated to cover up a sordid past and entangle the players in a web so confusing that no one could unravel the truth?

Valeria, desperate to rid herself of the blackmail but aware of the suspicion her actions might arouse, could have orchestrated the entire series of events. Her shooting Carter, her staged kidnapping, and even Louis's involvement. Maybe Louis had witnessed something he shouldn't have, making him a liability.

But where did Tilda fit into all of this? Was she just another victim of circumstances, or did she play a more active role in this drama? Her past as 'Blondie Swede' linked her to Carter, and her presence had complicated matters further.

As I sat there, turning the pieces of the puzzle over in my mind, my thoughts inevitably drifted to Daniel Hallstrom's involvement. Hallstrom, the renowned director, had a reputation that preceded him – a man of charisma and influence in the film industry, but not without his own shadows and secrets.

Could Hallstrom have been a part of the blackmail scheme against Valeria? It was a possibility I couldn't dismiss. The film industry is a labyrinth of connections and dependencies, and Hallstrom had the means and the influence to play a significant role. Yet, there was also the chance that Hallstrom was an unwitting participant, caught in the crossfire of Valeria's and Carter's dangerous game. His involvement might have been incidental, a byproduct of his association with Valeria as a director and friend.

But what truly gnawed at me was the question of motive. What could Hallstrom gain from any of this?

Was it all part of a marketing campaign for the new film? Or was he merely another victim in this elaborate charade?

I took a gulp, its cool spreading through me, bringing a semblance of clarity. Tilda's involvement with Carter, her past in the porn industry – could she have been the mastermind, using Valeria's secret to manipulate events from the shadows? Or was she another pawn in Valeria's desperate bid to protect her reputation?

The more I pondered, the more I realized that every player in this twisted tale had a motive. Valeria, to protect her career and reputation. Rocco, bound by loyalty and perhaps his own secrets. Louis, driven by obsession and perhaps a sense of justice for a star he idolized. And Tilda, caught in the crossfire of her past and present.

As I set my bottle down, I knew one thing for certain – this mystery was far from over. The truth lay hidden beneath layers of deceit, and it was my job to uncover it. Whoever was responsible, for whatever reason, I was determined to bring the truth to light. For justice, for closure, and perhaps, for my own peace of mind.

The sultry summer air clung to my skin like a lover's caress, seductive and suffocating in equal measure. I inhaled deeply, my lungs filling with the heady scent of sea salt and intrigue.

17:30, I glanced at my wristwatch.

"Time to make a move," I murmured, my words swallowed by the waves breaking on the sand, the shouts from playing children, and the shadows that still clouded this case. My Vespa purred beneath me as I navigated the streets, the wind teasing strands of hair from beneath my helmet, tickling my bearded cheek.

I parked in front of the opulent facade of the Grand Hotel Rimini, the playground of the rich and powerful whose desires were as insatiable as their appetites for luxury. I reached into my pocket and retrieved my phone, my fingers dancing across the screen as I dialed Commissario Carlotto's number.

"Pronto," came his gruff response.

"Salve, Commissario," I said, my voice smooth as silk. "Ferro here. I'd like to invite you to join me for a drink at the Grand Hotel Rimini."

A pause hung heavy with suspicion. "Why should I break bread with you, Ferro?" he asked, testing my resolve.

"Because I have uncovered something that will pique your interest."

"Very well," he conceded, the sound of rustling fabric betraying his curiosity. "I'll see you there."

"Va bene," I replied before ending the call. My heart thundered with anticipation, my blood pulsing to a rhythm only I could hear.

Entering the hotel's lavish bar, I chose a table near the floor-to-ceiling windows, where the afternoon light spilled in, casting a golden glow over the sumptuous velvet draperies. I ordered myself a gin with a slice of lime, savoring the bitterness as it danced across my tongue, igniting my senses.

"Signor Ferro," Carlotto greeted me, his sharp suit a testament to Milanese sophistication. He eyed me warily, his skepticism evident in the tightness of his jaw.

"Commissario," I acknowledged with a nod, my gaze never leaving his. "Please, have a seat."

"Get to the point, Ferro," he demanded, impatience etched into the lines of his face.

"Very well." I leaned in, my voice low and conspiratorial. "I've uncovered a connection between Valeria Bianchi, Rocco, her driver, and the blackmail scheme. But it goes deeper than we ever imagined."

Carlotto's eyes narrowed, his interest piqued. "Go on."

"Someone is pulling the strings, Commissario. Someone with more influence than any of us has noticed. And I intend to expose that person."

"Careful, Ferro," he warned, his voice laced with concern. "You're wading into dangerous waters."

"Ah, but Commissario," I said, a sly smile tugging at the corners of my mouth, "it's in those treacherous depths that the most elusive prey can be found."

"Please, proceed," he agreed, his determination mirroring my own.

"First, I need your authority to search one or two hotel rooms," I said, tasting the promise of retribution on my lips. I straightened up, my spine aligning itself with the steeliness of my determination. There was no turning back now. I would delve into the murky depths of deceit and desire, unearthing the truth behind each seductive smile and whispered secret.

8

The heavy curtains billowed gently as I opened the balcony doors, a breath of sultry evening air slipping into Valeria's elegant hotel suite. The room was filled with an atmosphere of tense anticipation, like the moments before a thunderstorm. Commissario Carlotto, Daniel Hallstrom, Rocco, Valeria, and Tilda had all gathered at my request, their eyes flickering between each other, betraying their unease.

"Let's not waste any more time," I said, pouring myself a gin with a twist of lime and settling into an armchair. "We're here to discuss this sordid affair – the blackmail scheme involving Valeria Bianchi."

My words hung in the air, heavy and foreboding, as four of them exchanged nervous glances. Valeria, in her silk gown that clung to her curves like a second skin, looked like she braced herself for impact while Tilda fidgeted beside her, her baby blue eyes darting around the room.

"For me, this started with a phone call from Signorina Tilda Larsson an evening some week ago. She begged me to drive out to Signora Bianchi's beach house to assist in a blackmailing case."

No visible reactions from my audience.

"As I came there, I witnessed Valeria firing a gun, rushed inside, and found the alleged blackmailer, Franco Carter, dead in a pool of his own blood."

I noticed Commissario Carlotto twitch as he heard this, which was news to him, but he did not interrupt.

"As I tried to calm and reason with Signora Bianchi, I was struck down, and she was kidnapped…" I looked at them all, meeting their gaze individually, trying to see their reactions. "But as this is in the make-believe world of movies, it was all pretend. Well, Carter being dead and me being knocked out was all too real." I managed a forced smile.

"I cannot know what happened just before I arrived at the beach house, but an educated guess is that Carter pressed Valeria for more money, maybe even threatening her with a gun…" As I said this, I noticed a slow nod from Valeria.

"Now enter an ex special forces soldier, living rough in a shack on the beach, and being an obsessed fan of Signora Bianchi. He hears the fight and steps in to protect his idol, killing Carter. Maybe he fled the scene, or maybe Valeria made him disappear. But he was not there when I arrived. As I stepped off my Vespa and killed the engine, Valeria fired a shot through the window to make it look as if she killed Carter—in self-defense, of course. I found the slug in a nearby tree."

"We cannot charge her for that," Carlotto interposed.

"True, Commissario, and probably not even for letting Rocco here hit me on the head."

Rocco moved his weight from one foot to the other but remained silent.

"One thing has nagged me from the very start: why did Signorina Larsson call me? As I arrived, Valeria seemed oblivious to my presence. She had not asked her assistant to send for me. Why did Tilda want me to go to the villa?" I continued after a short pause. "It took a new discovery to understand why. She wanted to protect Carter as she had been colluding with the late Franco Carter in his blackmail attempts on Signora Bianchi."

The room seemed to shrink around us as if the very walls were closing in. Desire, temptation, and betrayal hung heavy in the air, mingling with the scent of expensive perfume and aged leather. It was a heady mixture, one that threatened to consume us all. All eyes were on Valeria Bianchi, but she did not disclose a single feeling.

"Your secret's out, Tilda," I said, finishing my gin with a bitter swallow. "You can't hide any longer."

Tilda's lips parted, but no sound escaped. She swallowed hard, her throat working like a trapped bird.

Valeria's gaze flicked between Tilda and me, her eyes finally landing on the quivering blonde. "I... I suspected something after finding that photo in Carter's pocket," she confessed, her voice low and strained. "But I never imagined..."

Cornered and desperate, Tilda's hand shot to her purse in a frantic attempt to grab her small gun. With trembling fingers, she pointed it at me, her blue eyes wide with terror.

"You don't understand!" She shrieked, hysterical tears streaming down her cheeks. "Carter forced me into this! He said he'd ruin my career if I didn't comply. You must believe me, Luigi!"

"Drop the gun, Tilda," I shouted, my voice quivering

as Valeria's concerned eyes bore into me. Adrenaline coursed through my veins as I stared down the loaded barrel, helplessly aware of how one swift pull of the trigger could end everything.

"Please, Valeria," Tilda begged, pleading for any form of understanding or forgiveness. Valeria hesitated briefly, her expression torn between loyalty and disbelief.

Commissario Carlotto discretely slipped out his gun, jerked forward his arm, and aimed at Tilda's leg. There was a deafening bang that shattered the fragile silence and caused a searing pain to ripple through Tilda's body as the bullet found its target.

Tilda collapsed to the floor, her cries of pain echoing through the room as blood blossomed from her wound. Carlotto stood over her, his face a mask calm, the gun still smoking in his hand.

"You shouldn't play with guns, Signorina," he spat.

As Tilda writhed on the ground, I couldn't help but feel a twinge of pity for her. She had been seduced by the promise of fame, ensnared in a web of deceit that had ultimately led to her downfall. And yet, despite everything, she was just another pawn in this twisted game – one that had begun with a single, desperate act of betrayal.

"Grazie, Commissario," I whispered, my hand on his shoulder. "You saved my life."

"I'll probably live to regret it," he replied, his voice as sarcastic as ever. "What about the rest, Ferro?"

The wounded Tilda whimpered on the floor, her silky nylons stained an unbecoming crimson by her own blood. I took a moment to absorb the scene before me, my senses heightened by the weight of responsibility resting on my shoulders. The dark underbelly of the film world had swallowed her whole, and she'd become an unwitting pawn in Carter's twisted game.

"Listen," I said, addressing the room while keeping my eyes fixed on Tilda. "The truth is right in front of us. Tilda was involved in the blackmail scheme with Franco Carter. She used her position as Valeria's assistant to exploit Valeria for their own gain."

As if on cue, Commissario Carlotto produced a DVD from his jacket pocket, holding it up for all to see. "This was found in Signorina Larsson's room," he announced, his Milanese accent adding a layer of disdain to his words. "It's a porno... let's say exotic, test film starring Signora Bianchi, shot years ago when she was struggling as an actress. A film that ex porn-film producer Franco Carter had been using to extort money from her."

The revelation sent shockwaves through the room. Daniel Hallstrom recoiled as if slapped while Rocco clenched his fists, his knuckles whitening.

"You cannot prove I was part of this!" Tilda stammered, her Swedish lilt barely audible above the pounding of my own heart.

"The DVD was found in your room," I stated. "And Valeria found a photo in Carter's pocket of you, Tilda, or shall I say 'Blondie Swede' the porn actress?" My confidence grew with each word.

Carlotto raised an eyebrow but didn't say anything. Instead, he turned his attention to Valeria.

"Is this true, signora?" he asked, his tone curiously gentle.

Valeria nodded, her delicate hands trembling. "Yes," she whispered. "I found the photo after his death. That's when I started suspecting Tilda."

"Then that's settled," I declared, feeling an odd mix of satisfaction and regret.

"Then we have Rocco," I continued, my voice a steely whisper that cut through the tension of the room. "You've been awfully quiet through all this."

"Wh-what do you mean?" Rocco stammered, his muscular frame tensing beneath the crisp fabric of his tailored suit. The chauffeur responded to my probing gaze with apprehension, but he could not hide the telltale flicker of guilt that danced in his dark eyes.

"Rocco disposed of Carter's body at the old pier," I declared, watching as his face drained of color. "And later, when Louis became a liability... you eliminated him, too, didn't you?"

An uneasy silence settled over the room as all eyes turned to me, awaiting the revelation. I could feel their anticipation, palpable as the delicate silk of Valeria's gown brushed against her smooth skin.

It was Valeria who broke the silence, her voice dripping with venom. "How dare you accuse my driver of such a vile act!"

"Careful, Valeria," I warned, my voice dark as the shadows cast by the flickering candlelight. "You may not like what I have to say, but I assure you, it's the truth."

"Enough, Ferro!" Commissario Carlotto snapped,

his irritation as palpable as the summer sun's heat. "Your theatrics are tiresome. We'll handle the investigation from here."

"Of course, Commissario," I replied, my words dripping with sarcasm. "I wouldn't dream of stepping on your polished shoes."

As Carlotto bristled at my jibe, Rocco finally broke his silence. "I did it for Valeria," he confessed, his voice rough with emotion. "She's been good to me, and I wanted to protect her."

"Protection is one thing," I mused, my thoughts swirling like the velvety smoke of a fine cigar, "but murder is quite another."

"Enough." Carlotto stood his patience clearly at its end. "Tilda and Rocco will face the consequences of their actions." He gestured to his officers, who moved in to fasten cold, unforgiving handcuffs around their wrists.

"Very well," he said, turning to Tilda, who was still cradling her wounded leg. "You will be taken into custody and treated for your injuries. And as for you, Rocco…" He paused, looking the burly chauffeur up and down. "Your role in disposing of Carter's body cannot go unpunished, nor can your cold-hearted killing of Louis Celotti."

As the officers led Tilda and Rocco away, I couldn't help but feel a sense of closure. The truth had been revealed, and justice would be served – but at what cost? Valeria's glamorous world had been shattered, exposing the dark underbelly that lurked beneath the surface.

And yet, even in the midst of chaos, there remained a glimmer of hope.

"Yet another sordid tale from the world of cinema," Hallstrom muttered, shaking his head.

"Indeed," I agreed, glancing around the opulent hotel suite. "But sometimes, the most captivating stories are the ones that unfold behind the scenes."

For a moment, the room was silent as everyone absorbed the weight of the revelations. Then, Commissario Carlotto stepped forward, his face a mask of grim determination.

"Ah, Ferro," Carlotto sighed, his voice tinged with grudging respect. "You may be a thorn in my side, but you do have a knack for unraveling these sordid affairs."

"Compliments from the Commissario," I mused, my lips curving into a wry smile. "Truly, this case has been full of surprises."

"Before we end this," I continued, turning my gaze to Valeria, her dark eyes reflecting both fear and a hint of gratitude for my intervention, "There is one more piece to this twisted puzzle."

The setting sun cast a warm, golden glow over Valeria's lavish hotel suite, bathing the room in an almost ethereal light. I stood by the window, my gaze lingering on the breathtaking vista of the city beyond – a tapestry of ancient architecture and modern splendor, the perfect backdrop for our final act. I turned to face Valeria Bianchi.

"Signora Bianchi," I began, taking care to enunciate each syllable, "you staged your own kidnapping to create an alibi if you should be suspected of shooting

Carter, but also to create headlines." I paused, watching as her eyes widened with surprise. "Even if you cannot be responsible for any of this, everything has happened because of you."

Valeria's hands flew to her mouth as she gasped, her chest heaving like waves crashing against the sandy beaches. Her eyes glistened with unshed tears, but she did not look away. Instead, she met my gaze head-on, her chin lifted defiantly.

"Si, Ferro," she admitted, her voice barely above a whisper. "I did it to protect myself and my career... and the movie."

I could see the fear and vulnerability in her eyes, hidden beneath the veneer of sophistication and glamor. The shadows of her past clung to her like a silk robe, threatening to smother her with their dark embrace.

"Valeria," I said softly, my heart aching for the woman whose world had come crashing down around her, "your secrets are exposed now, but remember: there is still hope for redemption."

As she nodded slowly, I couldn't help but think of the business they were in – an industry steeped in history and culture, where desire and temptation had long held sway over the hearts of men and women alike. A place where power was wielded as deftly as a stiletto heel and where seduction and secrecy went hand in hand with the allure of Italian charm.

"Signor Ferro," Valeria's voice broke through my reverie, her husky, melodious tones tinged with bitterness. "I cannot thank you enough for clearing my name, but at what cost?"

She glanced down at the DVD that lay on the coffee table, its contents now public knowledge – the pornographic test film she had made in her struggle to make ends meet as an actor.

"Valeria, do not let that define you," Hallstrom interjected gently, placing a comforting hand on her shoulder. "You are an incredible actress, and that is what people will remember."

"Daniel, you are too kind," Valeria murmured, her eyes glistening with unshed tears. "But it is hard not to feel tainted by this... this sordid affair."

"Darling," Hallstrom whispered, his voice soft and soothing. "We all have our secrets, our moments of weakness. It is what makes us human."

"True," I agreed. "We must remember that beneath the veneer of glamor and beauty lies a dark underbelly that we can choose to leave behind."

"Leave behind?" Valeria echoed, her gaze searching mine. "Do you truly believe that is possible, Signor Ferro?"

"Si," I assured her, my heart swelling with a strange mixture of sadness and hope. "As long as there is life, there is always a chance for redemption."

"Perhaps," she sighed, a wistful smile playing on her lips. "But the road ahead will be long and treacherous, like the winding streets of a medieval city."

"Ah, but what is life without a little adventure?" I countered, offering her a rare smile of my own.

"True," Valeria chuckled, her laughter as rich and intoxicating as a glass of aged Barolo. "I shall endeavor to embrace the journey, no matter where it leads."

"Brava," Hallstrom applauded, his eyes shining with pride and affection.

With that, I knew it was time for me to take my leave, to return to the familiar streets of San Marino and put this chapter behind me. "Arrivederci, signora," I said, pressing a chaste kiss to Valeria's cheek.

"Addio, Signor Ferro," she replied, her voice trembling with emotion. "You have given me a second chance at life, and for that, I am eternally grateful."

"Until we meet again," I whispered, my heart heavy with the weight of our farewell.

With a final nod to Hallstrom, I turned and made my way to the door, leaving the shattered remains of their lives behind me. As I stepped out into the night, I couldn't help but reflect on the case that had brought me to their world – one of desire, temptation, and, ultimately, betrayal. The line between love and deception is often blurred – a sultry dance that lures even the most jaded hearts into its irresistible embrace.

And yet, for all its seductive allure, there was one thing I knew for certain: The truth, like the timeless beauty of Italian art, would always find a way to reveal itself.

*

The familiar streets of San Marino welcomed me like a warm embrace, their ancient cobblestones whispering tales of the past beneath my feet. As I stepped through my door, the chaos of the film world seemed to fade into the background, replaced by the comforting affection of Caterina.

"Luigi!" she cried, flinging her arms around my neck as soon as I entered my modest abode. Her laughter rang through the room like a melody, lighting up the space with its infectious warmth. "Now you have to tell me everything."

"Everything?" I chuckled, pressing a tender kiss to her forehead. "Caterina, there are some things better left unsaid."

"Ah, but you know how curious I am," she pouted, her eyes twinkling with mischief. "Especially about the film industry."

"Va bene," I sighed, recalling the seductive allure of the city I had left behind. The glamor and intrigue that had drawn me in like a moth to a flame, only to reveal the dark underbelly lurking beneath the surface.

"Tell me, Luigi," Caterina teased, her fingers tracing the hem of my shirt on the chest. "Did you succumb to temptation? Did the bright lights and beautiful women of the silver screen make you forget all about your humble life here with me?"

"Perish the thought," I murmured, wrapping my arms around her waist and pulling her close. "No one in this world could ever take your place, Caterina."

"Good answer," she giggled, peering up at me through her thick, dark lashes. "But I know you, being surrounded by all that passion and power…"

"Caterina," I whispered, surrendering to the warmth of her embrace. "Here, in this quiet corner of the world, is where my soul finds solace."

At that moment, as we stood together amidst the ghosts of our shared history, I couldn't help but think of the tangled web I had left behind – a world of desire and deception, temptation and treachery. And yet, for all its seductive allure, there was one thing I knew for certain: The truth, like the timeless beauty of Italian art, would always find a way to reveal itself.

The sun had dipped below the horizon, San Marino's ancient skyline was black against the sky. I stood on my balcony, sipping wine, and watched as lights from homes, shops, and restaurants went out one after the other. The city was about to go to bed, leaving behind a quiet rhythm that spoke of centuries of desire, temptation, and power.

"Luigi, amore mio," Caterina called from inside my modest apartment. "Come in and join me for dinner."

As I entered the dining room, I couldn't help but admire the soft curve of Caterina's neck as she leaned over the table, her fingers deftly arranging plates of steaming pasta and vibrant antipasti. Her simple dress clung to her body like a second skin, a far cry from the opulent gowns that had adorned Valeria Bianchi or the tight, short dresses that barely covered the seductive body of Tilda Larsson.

"Ah, Luigi," she murmured, her eyes twinkling with mischief. "I can see you're still thinking about your time among the glitterati."

"Perhaps," I admitted, my thoughts drifting back to the tangled web of deceit that had trapped us all – Valeria, Tilda, Rocco, and myself. It was a world where seduction and secrecy were currency, where loyalty could be bought and sold like fine silk. "But you must remember that the glitter is just the surface – behind the scenes lurks the dark underbelly that festers like a wound, hidden from view by a veil of glamor and beauty. And I'm reminded of why I prefer this life – a simple existence with you, far from the corruption that plagues our world."

"Then let us celebrate this," she said, lifting her glass of wine in a toast. "To us, and to the life we have – one woven from the threads of passion, loyalty, and the enduring beauty of simplicity."

"Salute," I replied, clinking my glass against hers. And as we drank deeply, savoring the rich notes of earth and sun that danced upon our tongues, I knew in my soul that it was here, in this humble sanctuary, that I would find solace from the shadows of temptation and desire. But for how long?

THE END

LUIGI FERRO
WILL RETURN

A Story from

Yesteryear's Stories Reflected Today
Yabot AB
www.yabot.se

www.ingramcontent.com/pod-product-compliance
Lightning Source LLC
La Vergne TN
LVHW020347200726
843507LV00012B/2535